THE PERFECT CRIME

"It's that simple, huh, Frankie?" Dewey was worried.

"It's that simple." I was telling the truth. The perfect crime was always simple, as simple as taking the money and not getting caught. Not getting caught was what we were working on.

"How come people aren't doing this all the time?"

"They don't think of it, Dewey. Bank robbers are hotheads. Some guy with a gun who needs the dough. It's a last resort."

Dewey gave it some thought. He rubbed his bare and muscular arms as if he were fighting back the cold.

"And I won't have no gun, right?"

"Don't need one, Dewey. That's the beauty of it. You don't need one."

"I just grab the bags and run up over the hill, then sneak to my car and drive away. It's not manly, Frankie, you know what I mean?"

"Who said crime was sexy? You want to fight bulls, go to Mexico and fight bulls."

HOT WIRE

Randy Russell

BANTAM BOOKS
NEW YORK · TORONTO · LONDON · SYDNEY · AUCKLAND

HOT WIRE
A Bantam Crime Line Book / May 1989

CRIME LINE and the portrayal of a boxed "cl" are trademarks of Bantam Books, a division of Bantam Doubleday Dell Publishing Group, Inc.

ISBN 0-553-18512-8

Published simultaneously in the United States and Canada

Bantam Books are published by Bantam Books, a divison of Bantam Doubleday Dell Publishing Group, Inc. Its trademark, consisting of the words "Bantam Books" and the portrayal of a rooster, is Registered in the U.S. Patent and Trademark Office and in other countries. Marca Registrada. Bantam Books, 666 Fifth Avenue, New York, New York 10103.

PRINTED IN THE UNITED STATES OF AMERICA

OPM   12 11 10 9 8 7 6 5 4 3

for Carol,
with thanks for the apples and oranges

HOT WIRE

What you want and what you get don't always come on the same bus. This was what my mother told me as a child, whenever I wanted something. Mothers are too often right. What I wanted wasn't coming in at all. What I was getting was burned toast and fried rice for breakfast, cold hamburgers for lunch and dinner.

I had gone to so much trouble, come so close to achieving my dream, that I could hardly believe I'd failed to grasp it. Yet here I was back in the hole, killing time in the Ottawa County Jail in Madrigal, Oklahoma. It's probably more accurate to say that time was killing me.

I paced inside my cage. I paced inside my socks on the concrete floor. The other thing my mother said was, "Wish in one hand and crap in the other, then see which fills up the fastest." What I wished was that I could fly.

Mom was right again. After three days the galvanized pail in the corner was filled almost to the top. I considered throwing it in the round, red-scrubbed face of the deputy who doubled as my jailer, but I didn't care much for hospital food. Especially when you had to eat it without teeth while fractured ribs kept you from sitting up in bed.

I'm Alton Benjamin Franklin, G.E.D. I was named after a hundred-dollar bill. I received my diploma from the McAlester State Correctional Institution in Oklahoma, class of '76. I lost a wife and a baby daughter in pursuit of my education. I was a busy young man. I had a business card once. It read: *No Reasonable Offer Refused.* You'd be surprised how few reasonable offers came along in a given decade. What I actually did for a living was steal things. I'd also sold paintings for a while. They were my own original Matisses.

If you're ever thrown in jail, use your allotted phone call to talk someone into bringing you a radio. Stabled horses are often kept with goats or cats to play with. They should have done as much for us.

I tried to sing but couldn't remember the words to anything, sitting there in my cage, so I made up the lines as I went along. Country songs, pop songs, rock classics.

I couldn't just sit there and brood on the old unknown world while the dark fields of my republic rolled on to the sea. So I danced around, practicing the variations of a fast-beat two-step. There would be plenty of time for brooding once I got out of that stink hole. Once I located Rosalinda. She was out there now, and I had the sinking feeling that she wouldn't wait forever. I danced faster.

The idea, as I figured it and as my mother would probably have told you, was that jail was supposed to give you time to reflect on how you got there. You got there by screwing up, and I'd already given that all the thought the topic would bear. It seemed a much more industrious mental exercise to use my time planning what I would do once I got out. Or perhaps thinking of a way to get out. When you're a thirty-year-old convicted felon, they no longer call your mom to come round and pick you up.

Sooner or later, I'd get free of the entire population of the great state of Oklahoma and start my new life as a success. All this, once I located Rosalinda. I'd never met her, but Rosalinda was by far the most important person in my life.

She was the remaining clue to the location of my missing four hundred thousand tax-free American dollars. It could have been more than four hundred thousand, much more, or a little less. I liked to think of it in round numbers. I liked to think of it as my future. I'd have new cards printed up: *Alton Benjamin Franklin, S.A.* This was me, self-actualized.

For the time being, though, I was in isolation with my unactualized self. A metal cot, a mattress. A cold-water lavatory sink on the back wall and my galvanized bucket. There was no pillow, no window. I wore my socks and jeans. And a clever tattoo of a colorful rooster on my left breast.

They'd taken away my shirt, along with my shoes. I'd been in and out of a few jails, and this had never happened to me before. Perhaps there'd been an article in *Jailer's Monthly* that described how an inmate had committed suicide by swallowing his shirt buttons. Not only was I without shirt and shoes (a state of existence that would keep me from being served in most restaurants), I wasn't allowed the comfort of bars to wrap my anxious hands around. Bars to look out through. My cell was a free-standing cage of interwoven iron slats forming even rows of four-inch squares. There was a wall at my back. I spent some of my time sticking my fingers through one of the square gaps to touch the crumbling, chalky plaster. It wasn't sable, but it was better than feeling nothing other than stale air.

The cage was erected over a drain in the concrete floor. I couldn't begin to describe the smell. When I'd first examined the drain, I'd made the mistake of placing my face directly over it. My knees buckled from the strength of the toxic odor.

"It could be worse," the deputy had told me when I complained. "They could of caught up with you in Texas."

They couldn't have caught up with me in Texas. I hadn't been in Texas. The car I was in, however, when I'd stupidly stopped for a set of flashing red lights nine miles south of the Kansas border, bore Texas plates. I'd actually stolen it from in front of a motel room in Sallisaw, just inside the Oklahoma line from Ft. Smith, Arkansas.

I tried never to take a car across state lines. In Ft. Smith, I'd abandoned a comfortable Buick I had previously picked up in Hot Springs. I hitchhiked across the state line. It was my method of operation. And it usually worked.

An outer door opened and closed. A familiar squeak walked in with the deputy's polished leather shoes. A ring of keys *jingle-jangled* his approach, sounding like a wind chime tossed by the breeze of freedom.

"Mail?" I asked, not standing.

"Supper," I was told. "Spread 'em against the back wall, you know." He inserted the key into the lock.

I didn't move. "I don't like hamburgers."

"Now, don't go gettin' moody," my Okie jailer advised. "Hamburgers is good food."

"Those damn things are neither hamburgers nor food."

"What you want and what you get don't always come on the same bus," he said, surprising me. "What you don't eat for supper you get for breakfast."

I quickly decided that I could tear the two burgers into tiny pieces and force them down the sink. I had begun to look forward to the burned toast and fried rice for breakfast. Somebody in that town knew how to fry rice. There were tiny bits of green onion among the flakes of rice. Tiny bits of ham. And just enough grease to warm the heart of a captured Confederate soldier on a cold train hurtling north. You didn't get rice like that just anywhere.

My mother was frying green beans in bacon grease when I decided to come out and get some. This was the way she told it. She called the doctor after reaching down from her skillet to feel my two feet sticking out. Breech.

I preferred to think that I hit the world running.

I stood up and faced the back of the cage, the plaster wall. I spread my legs and placed my hands over my head, palms against the lattice. The overweight Okie opened the cage door and set down my two hamburgers, welded to the paper plate, on the concrete floor. I relaxed and turned around to catch his shit-eating grin.

He stepped out of the cage, then turned to face me again. "Come tomorrow we'll bring out the hose to wash you off some," he said. "You're beginnin' to smell worse than a dead horse too many days in the sun." The door banged shut.

"Hey," I called after his fading steps. "You know all the words to any songs?"

Much later, I lay on my cot dreaming of the beautiful and unknown Rosalinda. "I'm coming to get you," I told the light bulb burning inside my cage. "That's right, Rosalinda, I'm coming to get you. And I'm coming soon."

You say something often enough, it makes it come true.

In the Ottawa County Jail in Madrigal, they turned the lights out at night. That and the fried rice were the two decent things they did.

I undressed for bed by taking off my socks. The cot was too short for my six-foot body and my feet stuck out over the end. Lying back on the thin mattress, hands under my head, I thought of the huge black roaches feeding at the open floor drain each night. I'd stepped on one the first night, Friday night, barefooted. And every time I ran water in the cold-water sink a couple of the big black babies came shooting up from the drain making a mad scramble for safety. I hoped they enjoyed the burgers.

In the sudden darkness of my cage, I swear I could hear the small beasts masticating their meal. A faraway door opened and closed. The building groaned. All I needed for a good cry was a whistling train to go rattling by; a Merle Haggard song.

I wiggled my toes, realizing that I smelled nearly as foul as the open drain in the floor of my cell. Nearly as awful as the contents of my galvanized pail. I hadn't shaved in four days. Tomorrow I'd ask for a bar of soap.

I'd also ask for a shirt to wear, warm from an iron and neatly creased. I'd ask for a pillow and a window and a moon in that window. I'd ask for a friend to be in there with me. A dog or a goat or a cat. I'd ask for what I wanted and then hang around to see what I got instead.

"Rosalinda," I sang out loud to the darkness, "you're first on my list. You're mine, beautiful baby, sweet baby, and I'm coming to get you." There was no place that woman could hide.

Chapter 1

It began the day I bought a suit. I hadn't owned a suit in years, hadn't worn one since my parole hearing in 1976. May 4th, 1986 the day before I turned thirty, I was sitting in my clean jeans and tennis shoes, my plaid, button-down shirt with the sleeves rolled up, in my five-year-old Datsun pickup truck.

I watched a young man from the suburbs park his car in a crowded lot just off the Country Club Plaza.

Maybe the kid was in college. He wore a white tennis outfit, a light sweater, cuffed and creased shorts over the tan muscles of his upper thighs. I wondered how in the hell a guy got so tan so early in the year. He carried his racket with him as he left behind a charcoal-gray Mustang.

There were a couple swishy places on the Plaza to eat breakfast. This guy was headed for one of them. The other shops didn't open until later. Gucci's and Neiman Marcus and Kansas City's own Saks Fifth Avenue. I made myself dislike him. I decided that carrying a tennis racket into a tourists' restaurant was asking to be taken advantage of. I always looked for a reason. It made me feel better at the end of a workday.

I climbed out of my truck into the light of a beautiful spring morning, carrying a brown paper lunch bag, and fed change into the parking meter. There was a two-hour limit. Plenty of time. I walked in the opposite direction of the parking lot I'd been watching.

I lived in an apartment on the Kansas side, but I preferred doing my work in Missouri. It basically was a

very decent job. I made a living. Like just about everybody else in America, I had to regularly get out there
and push a little money around. Carry a little money
from place to place. Moving money around is the way
we make our country work. I shouldn't have minded
working for a living. I named my own hours, which
were relatively few, and I didn't pay income taxes. I
never had guts enough to write in *car thief* as my
occupation on a 1040. So I quit filling them out altogether.

I stole cars, but never red ones. Red tended to
catch a person's eye. And contrary to the way they
behave, police officers generally fall into the category
of persons. Red or gray, however, the Mustang meant
green to me. My slim-jim opened the door's lock with
more ease than had I possessed the key. You just had to
love Ford Motor Company, if you were a thief.

I slid in behind the wheel and opened my lunch
sack. I removed a paperback book and held it open
against the steering wheel with my left hand. This was
the tricky part, getting the car started, and I wanted to
look as if I belonged where I sat.

While I read a few passages of *Burglars Can't Be
Choosers* by Lawrence Block, my right hand was busy.
My starter tool was no bigger than a two-inch lug
wrench with an adjustable ratchet. I locked the mouth
of it over the Mustang's ignition switch, working the
handle like a pump.

Piece of cake. Before I knew it, I was listening to
the irritating buzz of the seat-belt warning system. I
turned the handle in the other direction, starting the
engine. Quickly I removed the tool from the ignition.

While starting the Mustang, I never once took my
eyes from the paperback to see what my right hand
was doing. My right hand knew the ropes and needed
no guidance.

I removed the ring of keys from my lunch sack.
Each car key was filed to the point of being useless and
would slip into any ignition switch. Totally ineffective,
the keys provided the appearance of normalcy.

Sam Geolas told me I was paranoid to go to such lengths.

"What's it matter, Rooster?" he asked. "Either you get stopped or you don't."

But I believed you couldn't be too careful when you stole things for a living, especially cars. Maybe a turn signal didn't work. Or maybe the muffler dragged. I didn't want to end up in jail if some well-meaning traffic cop stopped me to let me know the brake lights weren't functioning. Police officers tend to notice things like a car running without a key in the ignition.

I pulled the Mustang onto the street and tuned into Kansas City's oldies station, WHB. I checked the odometer. I nodded at a fountain fashioned in the shape of a large carp with water gushing out its mouth. It was my favorite fountain in Kansas City.

The Mustang was last year's model and there were fewer than fifteen thousand miles on it. I was driving a five-hundred-dollar bill to market and I should have been pleased.

Instead it occurred to me that my entire life was a litany of loss. Other people's losses as well as my own. An unknown father, a dead mother, a high-school-sweetheart wife and a nine-year-old daughter. I'd made some friends along the way, but where the hell were they?

I was small potatoes. A guy doing good at being small potatoes had a porch by now, a woman, a dog, or at least a cat. There were small-potatoes vacations and retirement plans. I had none of that. And it came to me that I was small potatoes because I was afraid of being anything else. I was just getting by.

Turning thirty made me think about it. I didn't mind being thirty. I did mind the things I hadn't accomplished since I'd walked out of prison in 1976. I suddenly and very deeply minded that very much.

Something happened as I migrated north on a street one block east of Broadway.

There was a girl in a yellow dress, waiting at a bus

stop by herself. She looked at me and I snapped. Flipped. Crossed over. Came around. Hot tears filled my eyes. It wasn't a nervous breakdown exactly. It was more like a revelation. The woman looking at me had broken the camel's back of my mediocre soul.

I'd simply, at that moment, had enough of me the way I was. Things had to change. And it was up to me to change them. The thing I put my faith in was myself. I was now responsible, I knew, for my own salvation.

All this from a girl's looking at me. A girl in a yellow dress at a corner bus stop on the day before my thirtieth birthday. A girl who was a woman.

She tilted her lovely head and looked right at me while I waited for the light, and my life, to change. She almost smiled. I would gladly have donated my last pair of shoes to the Salvation Army to have known what she was thinking. The girl held her mouth as if to speak. I would have given up a high-paying career in avionics to water her plants.

The light turned green and the car behind me honked.

And I couldn't get caught in a stolen car. So I drove on.

Kansas City has plenty of trees and boulevards and parks. It has a decent zoo. There were baseball and football teams. Indoor soccer. There are skyscrapers and top-of-the-Crown restaurants. There is high-rent and low-rent. There are fine museums and burned-out tenements. It is a great town if you like to drive. So I drove on.

There were also two places in Kansas City that provided heart transplants. In case you ever needed one. I just drove on.

As with a woman, you never know a city until you've wintered with her. And not always then. Kansas City is a wonderful city in many ways. But I had been there too long. I wanted to move on. I wanted to leave behind all the excellent barbecue and move south for the next winter . . . with the girl in the yellow dress sitting next to me on the passenger's seat. But she was gone now.

As with all the other women in my life, I'd lost her. I couldn't remember my own daughter's birthday. She'd been born while I was in the McAlester pen. Her name was Avery and she was either nine or ten years old. And she, like the girl in the yellow dress, was gone.

I eased the waxed nose of the Mustang to within an inch of the garage door of the Good Buy Tire Store in the 1600 block of Broadway. I tapped the horn three times. The dented garage door lifted with a bang, and I drove inside between two racks of tires that were stacked to the top of the eighteen-foot ceiling.

A thin man they called Baron closed the garage door. I stepped out of the running Mustang, taking my useless set of keys, carrying my paper sack, and left the door open. Baron approached the car. He had dark, greasy hair that fell in his face. He nodded toward the small office at the back of the garage and climbed in behind the wheel. Baron floored it, listening for bad rings or valves.

I'd been inside the Good Buy Tire Store dozens of times and not once had anyone asked me if I wanted to buy tires. I walked to the back of the garage. Not hearing any problems with the car, Baron turned it off and followed me. I knocked on the open door of Sam's office and stepped inside.

Sam Geolas stood up from behind the cluttered wooden desk and arched his thick eyebrows. He was a large man with a large belly. His hairline had disappeared years ago. What hair remained he kept well oiled and combed behind his fatty ears.

"Mustang," Baron said. "I'd go five on it." He was standing right behind me, talking to Sam.

"Six," I said to the man behind the desk.

Sam Geolas nodded. I always asked for more than the initial appraisal. And I always got more. I brought in clean cars and was never followed.

There were a lot of kids out there who brought in some classic sports number after a hundred-and-eighty-mile-an-hour race on the freeway. I took care not to have a description of the car I was selling radioed over the police channel before I got there.

There were guys, too, who'd use the car for a date, planning to turn it over to Geolas the next day. They never lasted long.

Baron left. Sam sat back down in his chair with an audible grunt and lighted a cigarette.

"Rooster," he said, "when are you going to bring in the big one, eh?" He talked without looking at me and I saw no cause to reply.

"A Rolls or a Jag?" Sam brought out a plastic bank bag from a drawer of his desk. He unzipped the bag and removed a packet of hundred-dollar bills. Slowly, carefully, he counted out six C-notes. He replaced the remainder in the bag, zipped it, and returned it to its drawer. I figured there was a gun in the drawer as well. Sam left it open, his hand resting on its wooden edge.

"Maybe tomorrow," I said, considering it.

A Rolls is as easy to start as most other cars, just a little more difficult to locate in Kansas City. Sam lifted his gaze from the six bills he'd laid out for me and exhaled a cloud of blue smoke. We looked into each other's eyes as the last of the smoke drifted lazily from the nostrils of Sam's flat nose. I'd always tried to act as if I didn't hate the overweight, bald man with unfriendly eyes. It was getting tougher all the time and was particularly difficult today.

I almost didn't want to take my money.

"You know I go seven, maybe eight grand on a Rolls? Four or five thousand on a decent Jag?"

I nodded.

He studied me for a moment more then glanced away. I leaned forward, retrieved the money, and shoved it into my lunch sack. I was too busy thinking of other things to put much energy into shoptalk. Sam was right, though; it was time I did something different.

"There's an Excalibur driving around town. It's white. Has personalized tags. Kansas, ninety-nine. That's what the tags say, Rooster, ninety-nine. Know what that means?"

I shook my head. The Big One I had in mind wasn't some crappy car with personalized tags.

"Nah, neither do I. But I tell you what, mister, I'll go five grand on that one."

I nodded, said, "I'll see." I turned to leave.

"You're going to get caught. You know that, don't you? You guys always get caught."

Sam was laughing as I stepped out of his office. It sounded like someone coughing up concrete slabs.

"Hey, Rooster," he called after me. "Get you a big one sometime, before you get caught."

Outside the Good Buy Tire Store, the sun was shining and I tried to put the echoes of Sam Geolas's laugh out of my head. There were more important things to think about. My wardrobe, for one. If I was now going to take control of my future, my fate, and score the Big One, I would have to start out with a proper set of duds.

The kind of project I had in mind always began with a woman. And the one thing women still admired in this world was a man who spent money on himself, a man well dressed. I caught the Broadway bus, rode it back to the Country Club Plaza, and was in my pickup with nearly an hour left on the parking meter.

I drove to Oak Park Mall in the Kansas suburbs and selected a suit at one of the larger department stores. The suit was the same shade of gray as the Mustang that had paid for it. It was a tweedish number with proper lapels. A 42-long jacket, 34-by-34 slacks. I also found a pair of reddish-brown leather shoes. A couple of baby-blue shirts and a couple pairs of socks. A narrow red tie. It all came to just over $350. I paid cash.

I ate lunch sitting next to two large shopping bags

in one of Oak Park's fast-food places. It was crawling with young teens and preteens. Tomorrow was my birthday and being amid all that jabbering youth did little for my appetite. The food didn't do much for me, either.

I plotted my course of action as I drove.

I was a born driver. Motion cleared my thoughts, eased my soul. It wasn't uncommon for me, during times of anxiety or stress, to drive circles around the city I happened to be living in. My favorite drive in Kansas City started out by heading north on the Paseo, swinging over to Broadway once I was downtown, and then crossing the big Missouri River on the Broadway Bridge and heading out of town. At a convenient point I'd turn around and drive back. Crossing the Broadway Bridge at night going south provided you with a view of the city on the hill, lights dancing across the wide, dark water.

The way to rob a bank, I decided, was not to rob a bank. Of this much I was certain. A bank is designed to thwart successful robbery, right down to the exploding ink-packs they hide between the twenties at the bottom of the trays. A successful robbery is when you don't get caught. Then or later.

No one would try to stop you when you flashed a gun. It was the silent alarm that tripped you up. The marked bills. The cops waiting one block away to follow you onto the interstate, broadcasting your license plate to the highway patrol.

Like the rest of us and our lousy paychecks, banks moved money around. It wasn't all done by computer. Not yet anyway. Day in and day out, someone was out there moving the bank's money, federally insured money in staggering amounts. And it was already packaged for easy carryout.

I knew this from having met a girl from High Point, North Carolina. She'd been visiting Kansas City with her cousins. I'd joined them at their table at a bar in Westport. When she told me she worked in a bank, I told her I'd always wanted to rob one. She insisted that it wasn't all that difficult. I would turn thirty tomorrow, and it was time that I found out for myself.

Chapter 2

I pinned this project on a woman, and on my birthday I took my cleanly shaven, well-cologned, and impeccably dressed self into a bank. Not a bank really; a savings and loan association. Heartland Savings & Loan, to be specific. It had a clean, crisp ring to it.

"I'd like to open a savings account," I told the girl behind the counter after waiting in line for twenty minutes.

"New accounts are handled at desk one," she informed me. I began to relish the idea of taking this place to the cleaners. I stood around desk one until somebody showed up. The nameplate on the polished desktop let me know I was waiting for Wynona Krebs.

As life would have it, Wynona was a looker. Her dancing almond-colored eyes almost made her name sound good. She had a slight space between her two front teeth. It was the kind of thing that kept you looking at Wynona's mouth, watching her lips and tongue move. It was the kind of thing that made you want to give her one hell of a kiss. That, and the body trapped inside her dress. She was perfect for what I had in mind.

"May I help you?" she asked.

"Let me count the ways," I replied most charmingly.

She giggled. I was in. Her shoulder-length hair was that delicate shade of blond that looked red around the edges. And she wore no wedding ring.

I opened another savings account in my daughter's name. It was my favorite identity for legitimate dealings, complete with a valid driver's license and social security card. As I'd forgotten the date upon which the little darling had been born, I celebrated my lost daughter's birthday on my own. Today.

Wynona noticed the coincidence. "Happy birthday," she said.

"Thanks. Want to bake me a cake?"

"We might get something cooking," she said, thinking she was joking. Wynona liked me, liked my gray suit and my narrow red tie.

By now there were a few thousand dollars scattered in savings accounts in five different states in Avery's name. I kept a list I planned to use once I discovered where she and her mother were living. Avery and I would take a vacation together, stopping here and there to collect her college fund, her belated birthday gifts.

Usually I placed about half of what I received from a stolen car into an account in Avery's name or in the name of one of my other aliases. I stole an average of two cars a week. I lived on the rest.

Maybe it wasn't the best way to be a father, but it was something. This time I could only spare a C-note. The suit I wore had set me back a bit.

Two weeks later, Wynona still called me Avery. That was the hard part. She pronounced it in three distinct syllables.

"Thank you, A-ver-ry," she said, accepting the cold bottle of beer I handed her. We sat at a dinky table barely big enough to hold our drinks and an ashtray in a dark and dingy cowboy bar on Main Street. It was at her suggestion that we were there.

A group of bad musicians had finally taken a break, and there was a chance to actually hear what either of us might find to say.

Women who dress up for work, dress down for play. There was no figuring it out. Women who worked construction wore fancy underwear beneath their khakis. This was a not unpleasant discovery I'd made a couple years back. Wynona wore faded jeans that fit so tightly you could count the moles on her butt. A cotton T-shirt with the words *Rich Bitch* stretched across her braless breasts. Wynona's nipples dotted each *i* almost perfectly.

She also wore a pair of cream-colored cowboy boots I would have bought from her for my trips to the track if they'd fit.

"I just love country music," Wynona said, leaning into me. "It's so real! You know what I mean, Avery?"

I nodded. I grinned. "Call me Rooster," I said. I'd been saying it on a total of seven dates so far.

"It's about cheatin' and divorce and working for a living and stuff like that."

"It is that," I agreed. I sucked the lip of my beer bottle.

Wynona was ready for the second phase of our relationship. She made this clear when her hand found my lap and stayed there, resting like an animal asleep atop another animal. When one wakes, the other stirs. My animal was about to yawn, stretch, and rise up to see what was going on.

Even though it was a bar Wynona liked, I knew from experience that I had to get us out of there before the cowboys got drunk. I was a sitting duck for the regulars. Hanging around in the company of a bombshell like Wynona guaranteed I'd get my lights punched out before the bar closed at two or three in the morning.

Some barstool disc jockey played the jukebox.

"You ever drink schnapps, Wynona?"

A large man, wearing a plaid shirt with mother-of-pearl snaps, appeared from out of the dim recesses of the bar, like a cloud of ugly weather moving across a full moon. The look on his face was that of a man who'd either own the place before the night was over or burn it to the ground.

He asked Wynona to dance by tapping her on the

shoulder and staring straight at me. There was an un-
struck match wedged between his front teeth. Her
light-mocha eyes lit up like hundred-watt bulbs. It was
her way of asking if I minded. I nodded to the beer gut
standing behind her and Wynona got up to dance.
They took it at a slow swing.

I made my way to the bar and ordered double
shots of schnapps. I planned to have Wynona Krebs,
mild-mannered Kansas City savings and loan new-ac-
counts clerk by day and wild barroom two-stepping
cowgirl by night, drunk on her butt within half an
hour.

Chapter 3

Wynona was sitting on my couch. I tugged at one
of her boots. It wouldn't budge.

"You want to dance, Avery?" You want to dance
with me?"

I pulled and pulled and pulled on the boot. No
luck.

"You got any records?" Wynona asked this with
her eyes closed. She was toppling over sideways in
slow motion.

I considered getting the can opener from the
kitchen, then gave up on the idea of getting Wynona's
boots off altogether. I carried her to my bedroom and
dumped her on the bed. She said, "Oh," and passed
out.

I undressed and crawled under the covers Wynona slept on top of. So much for the secrets of bank-
ing. We'd straighten this out in the morning, I thought.

Later, I woke up curled on my side. Someone's
fist, I thought, was poking me in the stomach. The

radio was playing. I opened my eyes to see a cream-colored cowboy boot planted next to me, about half-way between my chest and my knees. It wasn't a fist poking me in the stomach at all. Above the top of the boot was a smooth, nicely shaped leg. A delicious-looking knee.

I rolled over on my back and bumped into the other boot. Wynona was standing on the bed, her hands on her bare hips. She was entirely nude except for the boots. She could have been smiling. I didn't lift my eyes that far.

Wynona later told me that she was generally happy and wanted to take a bath. An expert has said that happiness is a genetic disposition some people are born with. We'd made love. Or more accurately, Wynona had made love. I'd hung around to the end, but it was all her show. I'd never felt more removed. A part of me had been standing in the corner, watching.

Wynona was an investment as far as I was concerned, and there was nothing I could do to erase that fact from my thoughts. I didn't like myself for it, but she was happy and taking her morning bath. I told myself I wasn't hurting her.

Wynona was out of the tub much too soon, her body reddened from the hot water, her hair damp. And she wanted to make love again. She was insatiable.

I knew I had to act fast and get my new life on the road while I could still walk. At least, I told myself, I had a goal.

A goal? Okay, two hundred thousand little individual goals. But achieved all at once. One *Big One*. The annual earnings from two hundred thousand dollars, invested in boring but secure ways, was between twenty thousand and twenty-five thousand dollars a year. I could live comfortably on that. I'd even pay taxes if I had to.

I thought about it some more, convincing myself that I wasn't obsessed with money. I didn't even like money. If I could pull off the Big One and establish myself, then I wouldn't have to worry about money. It wouldn't be the focal point of my day, my week, my life. The money was going to free me from money.

I'd be free to do what I wanted to do, what I was supposed to do, whatever that was. I'd know once I had the money. It wasn't lust or mania; it was downright reasonable.

The next step was finding a patsy.

The kind of job I had in mind required a partner. Someone to do the time should, by some devilish quirk, everything blow up in our faces. Someone to actually pick up the money in his hands and walk (or run) away with it.

Moving the money to a hidden location was the critical act. It was the theft. It was the crime. I'd design it perfectly. I'd set it up and put it into action. But someone else would steal the money. That was my plan. And for that I needed a hired hand.

I'd met hundreds of people since moving to Kansas City from Wichita, which was too small to support my occupation but where my friends lived. Carolyn Sakowski and Paul Valley were my only two real friends on the surface of our entire planet. Previously I'd lived in New Orleans, Atlanta, Memphis. Places that rolled over and died after a year or two. Kansas City had lasted the longest.

I drove around in my pickup, my hands on the steering wheel like fingers pressed lightly on a Ouija-board planchette. I was guided by the magic of habit and happenstance. I found myself on the Paseo, my north-south, Kansas City, Missouri, boulevard.

It ran through more of the center city than any other parkway. I'd counted seven different parks along the Paseo and preferred to drive it south to north, from the glistening suburbs to the heart of the city. The Paseo runs more than nine miles from the promise of the future to the burned-out mistakes of the past, if you drove it like I did.

I drove by the Paseo Green, in the middle of

which lay a broad pool shaped something like an ancient Roman circus. It was fed by six small and dispirited jets of water. I turned around and drove back. Between Tenth and Eleventh streets, the formality of the Paseo past was preserved in a series of large arbors, built of concrete arms reaching across Doric columns. There were no vines.

At the intersection of the Paseo and Linwood, the Paseo for a moment appeared as grand as it must have appeared at the turn of the century. I drove between the ornate and ornamented Mid-City Towers on one side, and the grandly classical temple of the Scottish Rite on the other.

South of this, however, everything fell apart. The Paseo was cluttered with abandoned buildings and empty lots where buildings had once stood. The body of a sleeping man lay huddled on the steps to a building that was no longer there.

Driving the Paseo was my country music. It made me feel as though I were in touch with reality. I wished the politicians were each required to spend the night in one of those weed- and broken-bottle-infested vacant lots.

I continued driving. Most of the people you met in my business you wouldn't mind never seeing again. There were bars in town where the two-bit hustlers hung out, bars that catered to the cocaine crowd. The part-time gamblers and the addicts had their places to go. Dirty cops and softball teams. Old men from the neighborhood.

I avoided the bars. I didn't want a pro. And I didn't want an out-and-out loser. A pro would take it all for himself if I didn't shoot him. I didn't own a gun. An out-and-out loser would blow it. That is simply the nature of the beast.

What I needed was something in between those extremes.

The Datsun, as if guided by divine intervention, drove slowly onto the local campus of the University of

Missouri. A college student! Why hadn't I thought of that?

I parked. I cut across the grass. A starling lifted from the branches of a tree, swooped overhead, and lifted into a calm slide through the spring sky. I wanted to stay and watch the way he did that, but my pigeon was inside waiting.

The student union was buzzing with women taking themselves seriously and with men who refused to take anything seriously but women who took themselves seriously. The pool tables were in a room off to the side, a large room lined with electronic games. I spotted him the moment I stepped inside the noisy room. A red sign told me I was not permitted to smoke.

I was surprised to find that no one was playing the electronic machines. They chirped and squawked like a bunch of animals waiting to be fed. For all the noise the machines made, I'd expected a crowd of collegiates plugging away at the destruction of universes.

"Dewey Boone," he said when I told him my name was Rooster Franks. He said his name as if he expected me to have heard of him.

"Five a point?" he asked. "Rotation."

Dewey wore a black T-shirt, the kind that has a pocket just big enough for a pack of cigarettes if you don't smoke 100s. His black hair was thick and long, combed straight back from his forehead, over the tops of his ears. Dewey carried his cigarettes in a rolled sleeve of his T-shirt, trapped against a bulging biceps.

His hair could have been dyed purple and he could have worn a safety pin in the lobe of his ear; Dewey would still have been the guy I was looking for. A holdover from a former era. I knew him like I knew the image in my bathroom mirror. Dewey could have done real well for himself in small-town Oklahoma twenty or thirty years ago.

I watched his eyes carefully for a moment. He wasn't, I decided, a heavy drug user. That was important.

"Eight ball," I said. "Fifty the game. Lag for break."

While Dewey possessed a head of thick black hair, there was only minimal facial hair on his cheeks and chin. He wore a mock-mustache above his pouting upper lip. Dewey was bright enough, I decided, but he was wasting time, either flunking out or dropping out. Just hanging around, Dewey Boone was somebody looking for something better.

"You're on," he said, lighting a cigarette that dangled from his lips. I could have taught him how to make a decent living stealing cars. But I wasn't on the faculty.

I won the lag, made two stripes on the break, and ran the table. For the girl in the yellow dress, I told myself, I banked the eight ball into a side pocket. Dewey, as I'd already figured, didn't have fifty dollars.

Dewey agreed to take a ride. I snatched a wire hanger from the coatrack on our way out of the building. We walked along a sidewalk crowded with students. Class change. I tried not to notice the women. Dewey, however, turned completely around several times to scope them thoroughly.

"Where we headed?"

"Administration building," I said. "Where is it?"

"That way," Dewey told me, pointing right. A girl in red jogging shorts made her way up a slight hill. "Just follow those buns."

In the small reserved-parking lot behind the administration building, I approached a silver Mercedes 450SL convertible. I'd untwisted the wire hanger as we walked. Dewey followed two steps behind, looking first over one shoulder and then the other.

"Hey, Frankie, what you doin'?" he wanted to know.

What I wanted to know was why he called me Frankie. I already had enough names to keep track of.

A blue sign identified the parking space as being reserved for the chancellor. I had the door open with a flick of the wrist. I slid into the leather bucket seat behind the steering wheel and popped open the passenger door.

"Hop in," I called to Dewey. I slumped over and yanked down the wires from behind the walnut dashboard. Yanking was meant to add drama to the act. Dewey climbed into the other seat. He was nervous and he liked it. He closed his door softly.

"Come on, Frankie, what you doin'?" This time his voice was barely more than a whisper.

What I was doing was crossing the exposed portion of the red wire with the exposed portion of the white wire to fire the starter. The engine caught and I pulled back the red wire. I twisted the black wire and the white wire together in time, listening to the engine sputter, then catch again. I revved the motor.

Closing my door, I adjusted the rearview mirror, put the Mercedes into reverse and eased out of the chancellor's parking spot. We were off. It was a ridiculous risk, but it was important that I win Dewey over in a hurry. I didn't know how much longer I could keep Wynona happy.

I stayed in Missouri. In minutes we had the top down and were cruising along I-435, circling the city on the east side. North of town, about a mile short of Worlds of Fun, the local big-time amusement park, I pulled the convertible onto the shoulder. I let it idle.

With the traffic rushing by, I turned slowly in the driver's seat and stared hard at Dewey Boone. He fidgeted, looking straight ahead. I waited.

"What!" he eventually said, glancing at me then looking away.

"You owe me fifty."

"So what does that prove? I told you I don't got it."

"It proves that any imbecile can learn to shoot pool," I told him.

"Yeah, maybe so." He paused. "But I ain't no thief."

This time he looked right at me. There was a bit of lizard in this boy. A bit of courage.

"Maybe you should check into it," I suggested, patting the steering wheel. I pushed the silver convertible into gear and let out the clutch. I turned the radio on. The music combed our wind-tossed hair.

If I only knew then what I'd know later, I would have kicked Dewey Boone out of the car going seventy toward town. Instead I dropped him off at the corner of Sixteenth and Vine. Then I drove over to visit Sam's Good Buy Tire Store to sell him a set of used treads.

I went out the back door, turned up the alley, and crossed three streets to find Dewey leaning against the corner of a building, exactly where I'd left him. Curiosity was a strange cat. Anybody in his right mind would have caught the first bus by that corner and been gone by the time a guy like me came wandering back.

"You're cut's five hundred," I said. I handed him nine clean fifty-dollar bills. "Minus the fifty you owe me." I watched Dewey's eyes pop. His facial muscles flexed. His mouth worked nervously.

"Maybe I should look into this, Frankie." He put the money in his pocket. He'd done nothing to earn the money; what he accepted was a gift. And a gift was one hell of a responsibility whether you asked for it or not. But I didn't expect Dewey to understand that.

Chapter 4

Wynona made me anxious. Not in an urgent or devastating way, but anxious enough for me to rush things, to want to get on with it. She was too curious about my second bedroom, the one with the padlock on the door.

And Wynona cost me money. Where I'd gotten merrily along by stealing one or two decent cars a week, I was now bringing them in one a day. It was how I spent my mornings. Sam Geolas kept telling me I was going to get caught. He reminded me that I could take it easy for a month or two if I brought in a Big One. I was working on it, Sam; I was working on it.

I needed money for other things, too. Avery's college fund was near to doubling. I'd successfully befriended Dewey Boone. Just one more broad stroke of my brush was needed to win him over to the project. I wanted him to develop a quick taste for big bucks. For that, of course, I needed cash.

For that, we'd go to Omaha, where a favorite hobby of mine circled the track nine times a day, five days a week, this time of year. Omaha was one of the places where, when stealing things for a living got boring, I'd play the horses.

It was a little after ten P.M. and Wynona's long, blond body was in my bedroom, in repose. Lying in bed with Wynona, I said, "I want to talk."

"So talk. Go ahead and talk." She pulled her face back down against my skin at a place where my jockey shorts had previously been.

Fellatio was one sexual act I'd never been able to complete. My hang-up. I liked it, you bet. I liked it a lot. But when the time came . . . it didn't. You could say it had something to do with my mother, if you

26

were into Freudian analysis. If you weren't, you might say it had something to do with trust.

Either way, it drove Wynona crazy, and night after night she refused to give up.

"No," I said, pushing her head to one side. "I want to talk and I want you to listen."

"My ears aren't busy," she replied in a husky voice.

"Put your damned head on my pillow," I demanded roughly.

Wynona dragged the length of her body across me as she climbed back to the top of the bed. Instead of placing her head on the pillow, she put her bottom there, crossed her legs and sat straight up. Her back was against the wall that served as my headboard.

"What you want to talk about?"

"Just talk," I tried to explain. "I like to talk. It makes me feel human."

"You're funny," Wynona said cheerfully.

"It's little to ask," I said a bit spitefully.

I held myself rigid, staring at my closet door. I locked my jaw. Wynona could feel the knotted tension in the muscles of my arm under her hand.

"Okay, let's talk," she finally relented. "Tell me about your tattoo. How come a chicken?"

"It's not a chicken," I corrected her quickly. "It's a fighting cock. A rooster."

It was the kind of thing you had done to you when you were young and about to get out of prison. It had been my way of telling the outside world that I existed, that I would someday be at large. It had hurt like hell, especially the fill colors, but it was a pretty good bird. The old geezer who cut it into my flesh had had to mix nine different colors to do the job right.

Wynona waited for me to talk.

"You still want to talk, tell me about your other room," Wynona suggested. "The one with the lock on the door."

"I don't want to talk about me," I said flatly, brushing her hand away from my chest.

I waited for Wynona to say something.

"An old man was killed today taking out his trash," I said because it had popped into my mind. "Seventy-two years old, according to the radio."

"Who killed him?"

"It was this morning and a woman swerved in her car to keep from hitting a bus. She went up on the sidewalk and hit him. Dead. Taking out the damn trash."

Wynona said nothing.

"Everybody dies differently," I went on.

"I don't want to talk about dying," Wynona said. "It makes me lonely."

"Me too."

There was a long silence.

"Tell me about you," I said. "You know, what you like, about your job."

"I like you, Avery."

"How 'bout work?" I offered coyly. "Tell me more about the people you work with."

"You're funny," she proclaimed one more time.

Wynona did talk once she got started. It was up to me now and then to keep her talking about the specific person I needed to learn more about. Oleta Pryor was often asked to transport cash from the branch on Nall to the mother institution.

"The vice president's hosing her," Wynona gossiped. "Oleta gets all kinds of privileges like that. Driving around town in the middle of the day."

"Company car?"

"No, only the managers get company cars. They say she let him make a videotape of Mr. Foster doing it to her. Can you imagine that?" Yes, I could imagine it. And if I hadn't already come up with the perfect crime, I might have considered getting my hands on that video. It could have proved as valuable as the key to the Heartland Savings & Loan vault.

"Some girls get all the breaks," I said. "So she gets paid for driving around in the middle of the day?"

* * *

The next morning, a warm Saturday in June, I opened the sliding-glass doors onto my third-floor balcony and let the sun come tumbling in. Omaha was three and a half hours away via I-29. They loaded the horses into the gate for the first race precisely at noon. I'd told Dewey that I'd pick him up at eight o'clock on the dot.

I climbed into the shower, thinking of the girl in the yellow dress, thinking of the kids in the mall, thinking that in less than a month it would all be over and I'd be a rich man. On a slow week, Oleta Pryor drove to the main Heartland Savings & Loan on Thursday afternoon. If the cash, however, stacked up too rapidly, she made the drive on Wednesday.

By charter, it was required that the main savings and loan house the bulk of its capital resources, from all branch offices, over the weekend. They drew a nice interest rate by having the money in one place on Saturday and Sunday. On Monday morning they sent the money back out to the branches. On Mondays, though, it was a Brink's armored truck that made the deliveries.

I was pleased that over the past few years savings and loan associations had begun to provide many of the services previously available only at banks. Used to be a savings and loan didn't keep enough money around to cash a paycheck.

Now, it would be a few hundred grand. Minimum.

According to Wynona, that was the amount moved back and forth between the branch and the main office. Without being opened. A few hundred grand in clean wrappers. You had to like the regulations requiring savings and loan branches to have their money on the premises. Just like us, they were required to have the cash on hand when they wrote out their checks. Unlike us, savings and loan associations wrote out checks for the full amounts of new cars, business buildings, and fancy homes in Mission Hills.

I could manage, quite contentedly, on a few hundred grand.

As I stood under the spray of the hot water, the kids in the mall came back to me, and I wondered what I would do differently were I their age now. Not a hell of a lot, I decided.

I should have stopped the car and offered her a ride. I should have hopped out and stood next to her on the sidewalk and told her my name. My real name. Next time, I told myself, I'd find out what kind of things the girl in the yellow dress had on her mind.

Drying, I heard the distant humming of an unrecognizable tune coming from another room. I'd planned on leaving Wynona asleep in my bed, saying later that I hadn't the heart to rouse her from blessed sleep. We weren't on the best of terms anyway.

I'd woken up late last night to a series of sounds I couldn't identify. It was Wynona, always restless when she didn't have to work the next day, going through the cabinet drawers in the small kitchen of my two-bedroom apartment. By the time it occurred to me what she was up to, Wynona was already standing in front of the locked door to my second bedroom, my secret room.

Wynona was naked. She liked walking around the apartment that way and I'd never minded watching. Her arm was inside the room at the end of the short hall, reaching for the light. I stopped in my barefoot tracks. In an instant the hallway was filled with yellow light.

She stared into the room for the longest time, but didn't step inside to investigate. I pictured her blond eyes taking inventory, her brain working overtime to decide what the room was used for, what every little thing meant. What the paraphernalia added up to.

Sooner or later, she'd want to talk about it and that would be the end of me and Wynona. I prayed it didn't happen until after the bank was robbed, the savings and loan.

"Now you know," I said. "Hope you're satisfied."

Wynona had seen the contraptions of my secret life. She'd seen the tools, the whole setup. She stood there now, naked and apologizing, her expression aghast.

"Go ahead and pick up the key, Wynona," I instructed her.

"Lock the door and put the key back where you found it. Then get your bare ass back to bed and forget all about it."

Nervously she retrieved the key and locked the door. Then she attempted to walk by me on her way to the kitchen.

"Oh, Avery," she said softly. "I'm sorry. I just . . ."

"Shut up." I grabbed her arm with sudden viciousness as she came within my reach. I squeezed. She only looked at me, accepting my confrontation, my attack, as her punishment.

"You *will* never speak to me of what you have seen," I ordered, as a king orders the execution of a peasant. "You *will* never ask me a single question about any of it. Do you understand?"

Wynona could only nod, her eyes staring at our feet.

I released her and she padded away.

I should have known the sleepless bitch had been up to this. She'd probably searched a corner of my apartment every night until she found what she was looking for: the key to my secret life. *Dammit!* That life was mine and I didn't have to explain it to anyone. I slept on the small couch in the living room, chastising myself for having underestimated Wynona, for not having taken better care of the key.

Chapter 5

Wynona wore a summer outfit. She sat with one bare knee against me and the other resting against Dewey's jeans. Dewey found more room by sticking his elbow out the window of my pickup. He didn't seem to mind the crowding. I turned the radio up to keep everyone from trying to talk.

Occasionally Wynona placed both her hands on the gearshift knob between her legs and yawned. She wore sandals and painted toenails, pink terry-cloth shorts and a matching, tight-fitting sleeveless top. If she was wearing panties, you couldn't tell by looking. You could tell by looking, though, that she was braless. Her nipples threatened to poke holes through the cloth of her pink top.

Dewey was good about it. He ignored her. He must have decided I was emotionally involved. He must have decided that for the time being I was his friend. Eventually Dewey would catch on.

I picked up the *Daily Racing Form* at the Twelfth Street newsstand on our way out of town. I turned the radio off and had Wynona read aloud the past performances of the horses slated for the day's races at Ak-Sar-Ben. I-29 ran north through Iowa, along the Nebraska border.

It took Wynona a relatively long time to get through the races on today's card. But of course, she didn't understand a single statistic she painstakingly pronounced out loud to us. Neither did Dewey. He'd learn.

The three of us stood behind the home-stretch rail for the first race, listening to the thunderous approach of the racing thoroughbreds, listening to the roar of the crowd at our backs as one of the horses put his nose under the wire first. Wynona jumped up and down in her excitement, drawing the attention of several men around us as they turned away from the track to make final calculations before betting the next race.

"Okay, Frankie," Dewey said, "tell me how to bet."

Wynona had already devised her system. "It's purple today," she exclaimed, clutching Dewey's arm. "Today is purple. Show me where it says what colors the jockeys wear, Avery." I pointed to the line in the program that listed the design and color of the jockeys' silks.

"Bet purple, Dewey," she insisted. Wynona smiled and winked at him and I almost believed her myself. As she strutted off to place her wager for the second race, Dewey, and most of the others standing nearby, watched her walk away.

Actually, purple was the prominent color of the Van Berg silks, and Jack Van Berg was the leading trainer at Ak-Sar-Ben. Saturday was the big money day for owners, trainers, and jockeys. The purses were larger than on weekdays. If Van Berg was in the paddock, he was there to make money, and you could bet his horses weren't out there just for the exercise.

I explained the basics to Dewey. I showed him how to calculate roughly a horse's class by checking its past performances and the past performances of the horses running against it. I was in the middle of explaining the difference between a six-furlong sprint and a longer route that had two turns instead of one.

"Not that, Frankie. Tell me how you bet."

I paused.

"My number's four," he told me.

"Four?"

"That's my lucky number, Frankie."

"Lucky number?"

"Yeah, Rosalinda gave it to me. She does things like that for me. My lucky number's four."

"Who?"

"Rosalinda. She's got powers, Frankie. Some women do."

"Sure," I said. It was the first time I heard her name, the woman who would mean so much to me. I figured then that she was his aunt or somebody no more important than that.

"You walk up to the window. You tell them how much—say two dollars. You tell them the horse's number and whether you're betting it to win, place, or show."

Dewey stared at his program, studying it. The number-four horse in the second race was Careless Bet. A six-year-old gelding morning-lined at eight-to-one, Careless Bet had a chance, but there were better horses in the second race.

"Do it for me," Dewey said. "I'm nervous."

"Like this," I said. *"Two dollars on number four to win."*

"Just like that?"

"Just like that. Hand 'em your money and read your ticket to make sure you got the number-four horse in the second race."

"One more time, Frankie. Does 'show' mean coming in second, or third?"

Dewey returned with his pari-mutuel ticket. I was sitting out the first two races. Wynona showed up, jumping up and down with the excitement of a sure win.

"Careless Bet," she said. "Careless Bet." There were no purple silks this race, and Wynona had decided that pink was close enough. Don Pettinger, who was up on Careless Bet, wore a pink blouse and a lime-green cap. We watched the post parade. Careless Bet looked fit for a six-year-old, but the real standout was a dark brown four-year-old.

Hand Stand, carrying 117 pounds that included jockey Tim Doocy, was chomping at the bit, ears alert. Hand Stand was the morning-line and the public favorite. He was also the clocker's pick for the second race. I agreed with the experts.

"I bet number four to win," Dewey told me. "And I put two bucks on number eight and on number two to place. That's coming in second, right?"

I wanted to tell him that the only way his multiple wager would pay was if there was a dead heat for place. He should have put all his money on his best bet. It usually took a few dozen tries at combination bets to learn this, and someone's telling you such things rarely soaked in. I let it go.

Hand Stand was number seven. The four-year-old came out of the gate beautifully and took the early lead. Hand Stand and Tim Doocy were going for it wire-to-wire. The other horses looked like cows.

Coming out of the turn, however, Hand Stand stopped. The remaining eleven horses charged for the stretch, and you couldn't help but see the lime-green cap bobbing toward the front of the pack, moving between horses. Careless Bet won by a neck. Neither the eight nor the two horse was in the money.

Wynona screamed with delight. Dewey just grinned. Careless Bet paid $18.40. They weren't rich, but Dewey and Wynona were definitely happy.

The glow of his winning the second race was still on Dewey's cheeks after he and Wynona lost the third race. Wynona had switched to pink for the day, and Dewey hung in there, putting his money on number four.

I'd brought a bundle, prepared to bet the fourth race. I knew better than to bet on silks, knew better than to rely on some superstitious numerology.

The fourth race was a six-furlong claiming race for horses four years old and up. Keen Rajah, carrying the heavy weight of 120 pounds, was the morning-line favorite under jockey Tom Greer.

Dewey bet five dollars on the number-four horse to win. Doorway, morning-lined at ten-to-one, would be carrying only 112 pounds. He could have been carrying feathers. Doorway didn't have a chance. My bet was the number-seven horse, Loan Officer, a gelding running under veteran jockey Tim Doocy.

Loan Officer, going off at six-to-one, was carrying 116 pounds. From his record I'd decided that Loan Officer was ready to win. Every third or fourth race the horse stood on his ears and went for it. Doocy's silks were neon orange with an orange cap. I also had my eye on Wynona's horse, Keen Rajah, and a fifteen-to-one long shot, Chance Victory. Chance Victory was in the number-one post position.

Chance Victory and Keen Rajah were Loan Officer's only competition. Rajah was a speedball I figured would be hurt by the extra weight and the outside post position. Chance Victory needed a best effort to be up for the wire, but might do it.

The fourth race was an exacta. I went to the window alone. Picking the first and second horse in order guaranteed a big ticket in an exacta race. I boxed three horses for two hundred dollars a pop. The six separate bets to cover any order of Loan Officer, Keen Rajah, and Chance Victory cost me twelve hundred.

I put two hundred on Loan Officer to win. All in all, I'd wagered fourteen hundred on the race. If number four, Doorway, came in under the wire to win, Dewey would be ecstatic about his five-dollar ticket. I'd be unable to talk.

I stood behind Dewey and Wynona, keeping my wagers a secret, as the horses were loaded into the gate. It's the worst part of a race when you've wagered heavily. Loan Officer reared twice. I tried not to watch, but it would have taken a bolt of lightning down my back to distract me. I held my tickets inside a sweaty palm, my hope inside an empty and knotted stomach.

Keen Rajah stumbled coming out of the gate. Since he was a speed horse dependent upon a fireball start, the stumble probably cost him the race. Chance Victory, the long shot, shocked the crowd by taking an early lead under the urging of jockey Marty Wentz.

I searched the pack for Loan Officer's orange silks. My big bet moved into third along the turn, Keen Rajah at his tail. Doorway was a length behind Chance

Victory, but he faded at the head of the stretch. Dewey screamed encouragement to his mount, listening to the track announcer call the positions at the turn, unaware his horse had already given up.

Keen Rajah went wide for his run after the leader, Chance Victory. Loan Officer moved up on the inside. You could see Chance Victory tire as the horses reached the one-sixteen pole. My exacta was going to pay. Keen Rajah and Loan Officer caught and passed Chance Victory. Which of the two crossed the wire first, however, was impossible to tell.

If Keen Rajah won, my exacta would pay far less. Not to mention my two hundred dollars on Loan Officer's nose. It was a photo for finish.

Waiting for the photo finish to become official, I slipped my tickets back into my pocket and placed my hands on Dewey's and Wynona's shoulders. Wynona was trembling with anticipation; Keen Rajah's jockey wore pink silks.

Hearing the announcement, I was awash with a powerful glee. Placing an arm around Dewey's shoulder, I strode confidently to the windows. Loan Officer paid $11.40. My to-win wager was worth eleven hundred dollars in itself.

The exacta on the number seven and ten horses, in that order, paid $68.20. On a two-dollar bet. I had a hundred times that figure coming my way.

"Just a moment, please," the teller said after I pushed my two tickets under the window. She left and returned with the manager, who checked the digital readout on the computerized tote machine and then filled out a yellow slip of paper.

"What's going on, Frankie? You get caught cheatin'?"

"They have to get the money out of the vault," I told him, winking. He chuckled, but you should have seen his dark blue eyes pop and his mouth fall open as they counted out the money and handed it to me. It came to nearly eight thousand dollars.

"Care to place a bet?" the teller asked me. I shook

my head. I was through for the day. I knew how much
a win like this depended on luck. Some knowledge,
some guts, but mostly luck. Even the finest horses fell.

"Show me how to bet exactas, Frankie. Tell me
what I do."

"There aren't any more good races today," I said
solemnly, basking in my victory. Dewey would have
believed anything I said about the game. "Besides," I
added, "I got something else in mind."

"Like what?" he wanted to know. "Robbing a
bank?"

Wynona drank too many beers and put all her
remaining money on a purple-silked jockey in the last
race. She lost. Dewey had better luck. The number-
four horse came through in the last race, and Dewey
ended the day up more than thirty dollars. I should
have known then to ask him about Rosalinda.

Wynona fell asleep on the ride home. The sun
dropped out of view about halfway to the Missouri
line. We bought a twelve-pack and Dewey and I had to
take a leak about every thirty or forty miles.

Standing beside the Datsun on an Iowa farm road,
Dewey started talking. "A guy could make a living
doing that."

"There's only one way to find out if you're that
guy," I said, "and that's to give it a try."

"You, Frankie? You tried to make it playing the
ponies?"

"Busted my ass," I said honestly.

"You were lucky today, huh?"

"Yeah, lucky. It's a lot of work to stay lucky,
Dewey. A lot of discipline." I wanted to say that the
only luck at a racetrack was bad luck. When you lost, it
was bad luck. When you won, it wasn't luck at all; you
had it figured. At least that's the way it was before you
lost a hell of a lot of races you should have won. Then
you realized the pays *were* luck and then it was over.
The horses beat you. They broke your butt and they
broke your heart. You were better off betting on love.

"You bet those other races, didn't you, Frankie?"

I hadn't. I let Dewey think what he wanted to think as we watered the darkened Iowa landscape. The secret to winning more that you lose playing the horses might have been in picking your races as carefully as you picked your horses. Some pros go for days of intense study and detailed observation without placing a wager.

"Two hundred a pop, Frankie. I like that. You're really something. Did you end up giving some of that money back, or what?"

I said nothing. On the way back to the truck Dewey surprised me by handing me his winnings: his forty-two dollars.

"I owe you this," he said almost shyly. "And eight to go. A man's got to pay off his bets or he isn't a man."

I accepted it. The night surrounded us. The radio played inside my Datsun pickup. Wynona slept. It was me and Dewey alone in the night of endless stars. Alone with the future. We could have, at that moment, climbed into my little truck and driven anywhere. El Salvador was just around the next corner.

We stood side by side, looking out over the fields. It was now or never.

"You said something earlier about robbing a bank, Dewey. You remember?"

Chapter 6

Wynona went to church. Dewey showed up about ten minutes later at my place to go over the details.

"It's that simple, huh, Frankie?" Dewey was worried.

"It's that simple." I was telling the truth. The perfect crime was always simple, as simple as taking the money and not getting caught. Not getting caught was what we were working on.

"How come people aren't doing this all the time?"

"They don't think of it, Dewey. Bank robbers are hotheads. Some guy with a gun who needs the dough. It's a last resort."

"Some guys like it, I hear."

"Danger and violence," I said sourly. "Who needs danger and violence?"

"Lots of jerks do." It was Dewey's turn to be right.

"And that's why they don't think of it in any other terms."

Dewey gave it some thought. He rubbed his bare and muscular arms as if he were fighting back the cold.

"And I won't have no gun, right?"

"Don't need one, Dewey. That's the beauty of it. You don't need one."

"It's so pussy," he finally declared. "I just grab the bags and run up over the hill, then sneak to my car and drive away. It's not manly, Frankie, you know what I mean?"

"Who said crime was sexy? You want to fight bulls, go to Mexico and fight bulls."

I paused. Everyone thought crime was sexy. Cops and robbers were sexy. Violence, especially violent death, was sexy. Guns were sexy. Stealing fast cars was sexy. I was beginning to tire of Dewey's being right about these things.

"You want macho or money, Dewey? You want macho, get yourself a gun and drive to the nearest filling station. You want money, you help me do this pussy thing here I got all worked out."

Dewey Boone rubbed his chin. He ran a hand through his thick black hair. He found a cigarette and lighted it. Dewey was everything I'd expected him to be, and a little bit more. Eventually he got around to it.

"What keeps me from driving off and leaving you with nothin'?"

"You're afraid to." This time I was right. "You're

afraid to have the whole show on your head from that day on. You need me to carry half the load, Dewey. You're virgin and you can't handle it. You'd get caught."

He didn't like what I was saying. Afraid I might be accidentally challenging him to what he wouldn't normally do, I added a warning.

"Besides, all I have to do is talk. There are people who'd go to a lot of trouble to find a man hiding out with a couple hundred grand."

He exhaled his cigarette smoke and looked at me.

"And you're afraid of me," I added.

"Now you're talking, Frankie."

I decided to give Dewey all the machismo he demanded in order to feel good about our partnership.

"Because I'm crazy and I'd find you and I'd kill you, Mr. Boone. Yes, I believe I would. I'd cut your throat and pull your tongue out the slit like a necktie."

Dewey was suddenly game. He grinned.

"It might be fun," he admitted. "Hey, I got this uncle that lives in Hot Springs, you know, down in Arkansas. And they got this racetrack there. I've never been to the races there, but maybe you and me could hit the road after and sort of check it out. You know, in high style."

I waited an extra beat.

"Not on your life," I replied harshly. "You and I have to stay in town. We keep doing what we've been doing. I have to keep seeing Wynona for a while, and you have to go straight back to that student union pool table. You listening to me, Dewey? You better be, because this part's important."

"Okay, okay, Frankie," he said with a wave of his hand.

But I wasn't finished.

"Running for cover is when you get caught. They catch you at the airport, Dewey. It happens all the time, you read the papers."

"You're right, Frankie. Yeah, you're right. It's just that I never had any money before. It kind of makes me want to go somewhere . . . but I'll stay put for a while. You've set this thing up, Frankie, and I'll go along."

"A contract, Dewey. Think of it as a contract. A business deal and we're partners. I go down the shithole, you go down the shithole. I prosper, you prosper. A contract."

"Where do I sign?"

We talked it through again and again. Before Dewey left, he asked me about my secret bedroom.

"What you got locked up in there, anyway? Hey, Frankie, you making hundred-dollar bills to bet on the horses?"

"Something like that," I said. "I'm a man of many talents."

Razzle-dazzle, there was none. On Monday, Dewey and I drove through a dry run. I showed him the branch Heartland Savings & Loan on Nall Avenue and Sixty-third, the Johnson County suburbs. I showed him the orange Toyota station wagon that belonged to Oleta Pryor. I showed him the route I'd take in whatever car I would be driving then.

I showed him the vacant sloping hill he'd come running down. I showed him the spot among the blue oaks at the top of the long hill where I wanted him waiting. I showed him the neighborhood behind the hill and a place to park his car. We drove by the thick brush on the neighborhood side several times. I told him he would not, under any circumstances, be wearing a mask. Or carrying a gun.

The sunlight glinted off the hood of my pickup as I drove Dewey to the parking garage at the University of Kansas Medical Center, where he'd load the money into the trunk of his car, go into the hospital cafeteria, and eat something. Then he'd come out and drive the car to the Woodside Racquet Club, lock it up, and walk away.

"You can do that, Frankie? You can get her to stop right there?"

"Right there." I pointed to the spot as we drove back toward the Heartland Savings & Loan branch.

"But I won't know what car you're in," he protested. "What if somebody else hits the wagon?"

"It would be God's way of helping us out, Dewey."

"Yeah, Frankie, the Old Guy just has to hate bankers, I know that much." Dewey laughed, but it was a nervous laugh. There were a hundred ways fate could screw us, and it didn't do the nerves a whole lot of good to bring them up.

That night I took Wynona out to eat. Growing nervous, too, I was quite capable of eating myself into a frenzy. At the North China Restaurant on Broadway, I ordered the slowest thing on the menu: Peking duck. Wynona thought that was terribly sweet of me, because the duck was also the most expensive thing on the menu.

We slurped out egg drop soup.

"Avery?" she said, looking up at me with her blond eyes. "What do you do for a living?"

"Daddy's rich. He sends me money."

"Yeah"—she looked into her soup— "sometimes you seem to have quite a lot."

"Lack of discipline. I'm a spendthrift."

"How come you don't dress like you got money?"

Next, she was going to make fun of my pickup. "It embarrasses me."

Wynona giggled. She wasn't too sure about that. "You want to get dressed up in your suit one night soon and go out fancy? Avery, I think I'd like that."

"Let's see what's in your fortune cookie first." I burned the ceiling of my mouth on a too-large spoonful of soup.

"You'd look real good in a cowboy hat," she said from out of nowhere. "And alligator boots."

And a few pounds of tooled Mexican silver around my neck and wrists, I thought. I found myself now wishing the food would hurry up and get there. What the hell had I been thinking when I'd ordered Peking duck?

My nerves were taut and I knew what I needed.

"You know what I could use tonight, Wynona? I could use a good drunk."

Wynona smiled knowingly. Her blond eyes danced. It was something someone like Wynona Krebs understood.

"You take care of me if I get real stinking-assed polluted?"

"You know I will, Avery. Everybody needs that once in a while."

"I wouldn't want you to miss work or anything."

Wynona assured me she needed little sleep.

"You won't run off with somebody else and leave me in a gutter somewhere?"

"Avery!" she snapped. "You know better than that."

With women, sometimes you had to come right out and ask for what you wanted. What I wanted more than a drunk was a hangover. A hangover hurt, but it always proved the perfect purge. It would clear my mind and eventually steady my nerves.

Tuesday afternoon I apologized to Dewey for not letting him turn on the radio.

"What the fuck you doing all messed up?" he wanted to know.

"Had to get it out of my system." We were driving our route for the fifth time that day.

"Frankie," he said, shaking his head and pointing at a stop sign, "sometimes I worry about you. Tomorrow is the biggest day of my life and here you are all fucked up!"

"Dewey," I said, "sometimes so do I."

I cut myself shaving. I couldn't find the right socks. The elastic in my underwear broke. Dewey was in the other room, trying to force himself to listen to the stereo. He'd showed up the minute Wynona left for work. He said he'd been unable to sleep and had spent the night in his sister's car, watching my apartment building.

"You're not making it easy," I informed him. "You should be sleeping in late or taking a long, hot bath."

"You're crazy, Frankie, you know that?"

I stood in the doorway of the bathroom, wearing my jeans and towel-drying my hair. For the first time I began to worry about Dewey Boone.

"Where's your cool?" I asked him, almost shouting. "Where's your poolroom cool, Dewey?"

He just looked at me, like a freeze-frame on a video of somebody talking, caught between his words, trapped between thoughts.

I snapped off the stereo. Dewey continued to stare as I marched to a position just inches in front of him. I placed my hand on his shoulder. He looked as if he wanted to punch me in the face.

"I need you," I told him. "You find your cool, okay? I need the Dewey Boone I met hanging on a pool cue that day. He's right *there*, Dewey." I poked his chest with a finger. If he wanted to take a swing at me, he might as well get it over with.

"He's right in there," I went on. "And you'd better find him quick or this whole thing's going to blow up in your face and I'm going to walk away whistling 'Dixie.'"

He calmed a little.

"You can count on me," Dewey finally said, audibly exhaling.

Actually, Dewey's nervousness helped me to control my own. He sat down on the couch and found a cigarette. He held it in his hand, his hand in his lap.

"I'm sorry, Frankie. It's just that I ain't ever done anything this big."

Me too, kid, I thought. Me too.

I turned WHB back on to discover that any number of fools still fell in love. In my bedroom I put on a button-down striped shirt. I put on my jogging shoes. I wondered what in the hell Dewey and I were going to do to pass the time. At one o'clock I'd drop him off. I'd find a car. I'd be waiting at two o'clock. Oleta made her drive, her short and profitable drive, between two and three. Once a week always between two and three.

I wondered what kind of shape we were going to be in if Oleta Pryor wasn't asked to courier that few hundred grand till tomorrow.

"I've got it," I said, coming back into the front room. Dewey exhaled an upward-flowing river of smoke. "Let's walk the Plaza and figure out what we'd buy with the money."

Dewey smiled. He liked that. "Yeah, Frankie, let's go to Gucci's."

"Bonwit Teller. Tiffany's. Saks Fifth Avenue."

"You got it!"

It would be the perfect way to work off the tension—walking, being around people . . .

Later, Dewey sat among the blue oaks at the top of the hill along Nall Avenue, while I listened to the radio in a stolen '78 Ford station wagon. The big, ugly car, pitted with rust, would serve just fine as a battering ram.

But I didn't get to try it. I watched the parking lot at the Heartland Savings & Loan with such intensity that I began to hallucinate small animals running under the cars parked there. Animals that peeked out at me. By three-thirty I knew it wouldn't happen that day.

Chapter 7

The one thing I hadn't practiced was wrecking the car. I worried now that I might slam into her Toyota too hard. That I might knock myself out, or by some quirk kill myself. I didn't want to die almost as badly as I wanted to pull off the Big One. Almost.

I wore my gloves. It was to be a nice, clean crime. I toyed with the mock keys in the Pontiac I'd stolen not more than twenty minutes ago and tried to read my paperback. I tried, too, not to stare at the orange station wagon parked behind the Heartland Savings & Loan branch on Nall at Sixty-third Street. At ten minutes after two on a fine Thursday afternoon, I was coiled like a spring, being pulled tighter and tighter by every second I was forced to wait.

There was absolutely nothing to think about but the things that could go wrong.

Naturally, the thing that would go wrong I didn't even consider. He was on the grassy hill, three blocks up Nall Avenue, experiencing his own gambler's trauma. Smothering under his own sweaty blanket of nervous hell.

Leave it to me, I thought, to steal a car with a broken radio. I felt inside my lunch sack for the medicine bottle I'd brought along. For the three-hundredth time it was there.

I was scared. The stakes were too high.

Two security guards finally appeared. They loaded four canvas bags into the rear hatch of Oleta Pryor's station wagon. They covered the bags with a blanket as if the bags were illegal aliens on their way across the border. They closed the lid. The three of us waited.

Oleta showed up. She chatted with them as she

opened the driver's door and climbed in behind the wheel. The orange wagon backed out of its reserved parking space. The race was on.

I pulled up to the stop sign on Nall. She'd pass me in a moment and I'd pull in right behind. It was a simple right turn. But I had to wait for two cars already behind Oleta. They weren't about to pass her either and get out of my way. Oleta drove as if heatedly pursued by Atilla, king of the Huns.

"Slow down, you bitch," I said to the cracked windshield as I squealed the Pontiac's tires getting onto Nall Avenue. Within a block I was behind her and the other two cars were falling back. It occurred to me only then that traffic might add a touch of mayhem to my carefully planned collision. The excitement built. I could feel my blood speeding up as it ran its course under my skin.

We were through one intersection. It was happening too fast. We were already in the middle of block two. I changed lanes.

I moved the big green Pontiac alongside the Toyota wagon as we drove through the second intersection a full fifteen miles an hour over the speed limit. Oleta Pryor was singing to the radio.

I accelerated, bringing the tip of the Pontiac's hood even with the driver's door of the small station wagon. I didn't want Oleta to glance over at me and have my face indelibly imprinted on her memory.

The moment was upon us. I jerked the steering wheel hard to the right, pushing the Pontiac into the moving rear door of Oleta's orange station wagon. Simultaneously I slammed on the brakes.

Prepared for the jolt, I was surprised by the noise. The crunch of metal sounded like a hammer crushing my teeth, magnified by ten. My brakes locked and screamed. The tires smoked. And Oleta Pryor drove off the road and into the ditch at the bottom of Dewey Boone's hill topped by the cluster of towering blue oaks.

I wanted both of us to come to a stop in the ditch.

Oleta, not knowing what hit her, stamped on the brakes like a good girl and ended up where she should. I, however, having let up on the brakes when they locked, ended up with a hot wind in my face. The green Pontiac's heater had come on full blast upon contact with Oleta's Toyota. I reminded myself never to steal another used Pontiac.

I stopped too far away, my car sideways in the intersection.

I gunned it, spinning sideways on smoking tires, and pulled into the ditch from the opposite direction. Racing through the grass and the mud, I then braked the Pontiac, the tip of its bumper coming to a stop against the front bumper of Oleta's wagon. I hopped out before anyone else could stop to help. Glancing to my left, I caught a glimpse of Dewey coming down the hill in a dead run. He appeared no more out of place than a pedestrian rushing to the aid of strangers.

Except that Dewey carried a gunnysack.

Except that he opened the hatchback of the wagon before checking on the driver.

Except that he loaded four canvas bags into his burlap sack.

Except that he was turning now to dash back up the long hill and toward the watching trees with his burden.

In my surgical-gloved hand I held a small bottle of chloroform, but I needn't have bothered. She was out cold, slumped over in the seat. I heard a car door slam. I looked up in time to see Dewey Boone disappear between two blue oaks at the top of the hill, and to see a man in his gray-haired fifties running toward me.

I glanced back up to the trees and could see nothing but the breeze-rattled leaves bouncing green light back to me. The grass where Dewey's heavy steps had trod rose up slowly in the sunlight to cover his tracks. The image of Dewey's disappearing over the hill was akin to a religious vision and I wanted to sit down and savor it. But I had my job to do.

I had my gloved hand on Oleta's wrist, pretending

to check her pulse through the stretched latex covering my fingers. All I could feel was my own pulse
beating a savage music against my temples. I could see
no blood, however, and it appeared as if Oleta had
merely suffered a bang on the noggin.

"Help this poor woman!" I screamed to the man
approaching us, now no more than a few feet away. I
spun on my heels before he could bother to get a good
look at me, his eyes searching the interior of the station wagon for signs of carnage. "She's dying," I called.
"I'll get an ambulance on the way!"

I carried my unneeded bottle with me, jumped
into the still-running Pontiac and backed away from
the scene of the accident. The scene of the crime.
Another car was stopping. Who were all these good
people, I wanted to know, coming to the aid of their
fellowman?

It didn't matter. If anyone caught a tag number, it
wasn't mine in the first place. And no one but Dewey
Boone and I had any idea that the bank had just been
robbed. And of course, Oleta Pryor whenever she
came to.

I drove toward State Line Road on Sixty-third
Street, my heart going ninety, the dark-green Pontiac
a measly fifty-five. I was driving straight into my
golden, cash-filled future, concentrating to get
through the remaining steps of my simple if unmanly
plan.

Chapter 8

Dewey hadn't closed the hatchback. The image of the rear-opened orange Toyota station wagon burned in my head. Like a woman raped, I carried the slow-motion events and images of the crime with me, locked inside a chain-saw headache as I paced from room to room in my apartment. There was nothing wrong with me that a five-mile swim wouldn't cure.

I rubbed my chin. Modern science should look into the effect of stress and excitement on beard growth. I badly needed a shave. And I badly needed to know how Dewey Boone had faired. I had an avid interest in that. An overriding concern.

The phone rang.

He wasn't supposed to call. I dashed into the bedroom and leapt onto the bed, reaching for the Trimline on the bedside table near the opposite wall. I picked it up on the first ring. Modern science should look into people's moving faster than the speed of sound.

It was Wynona. She was breathless.

"You're kidding?" I feigned dramatically. "Really?"

She told me all about it. How three men with machine guns, or some such nonsense, had forced Oleta Pryor off the road. How they'd driven off in a van with darkly tinted windows and with at least four hundred thousand dollars of Heartland Savings & Loan's favorite asset.

"Four hundred thousand?" I asked, my curiosity as real as real could be.

"Probably more is the rumor around here. They say banks always lie about the amount. Ada thinks it could be more like a half million. Can you believe it?"

51

I wanted to believe it. My stomach fell to my knees with the thought of it. I had yet to consider the money as a sizable fraction of a million dollars. Dewey was to get twenty percent. That left me with about a third of a million dollars. This was the Big One indeed. I'd never have to look at Sam Geolas's yellow-toothed sneer again.

"Well, she should know," Wynona continued. "Ada's in Accounting."

I wished I'd have known then that I'd be in the Ottawa County Jail before I talked again to Wynona Krebs. I would have made up an excuse for her to believe and to repeat to the detectives who would eventually interview her. At the time I thought she'd get through it okay and she probably would. Wynona had no reason to think I had a thing to do with it.

It was Oleta Pryor's background the dicks were going to dig into. Hers and Mr. Foster's. It was his own fault. A man should know better than to shit where he eats. That's what my mother would have said.

I turned on the radio and stripped. I shaved for the second time that day. I stepped from the shower to discover I'd made the news.

I gloated briefly.

"WHB Newswatch has just learned that a savings and loan courier was robbed this afternoon as she carried deposits from a branch office of the Heartland Savings & Loan at Sixty-third and Nall Avenue. The courier was injured in the robbery, in which it was reported that three masked men carrying weapons forced the courier's car into a ditch along Nall Avenue.

"Oleta Pryor, who routinely delivered large sums of money to the savings and loan home office, was treated and released at Shawnee Mission Hospital. The alleged robbers were reported to have driven away with more than four hundred thousand dollars Miss Pryor was carrying in her privately owned vehicle. More at the top of the hour."

Radio stations got their news breaks by monitoring the police bands over the shortwave radio. If anyone had been arrested as a suspect, they'd know about at the same time headquarters learned of it. Tomorrow the police would have a code name for the robbery. Today, they were still playing it by the numbers. And even a cub reporter knew the difference between a "ten-four" and a "ten-thirty-one."

Apparently the police believed it was a hit-and-run robbery. That I had taken the money. They had no reason to suspect an accomplice.

By now Dewey would be leaving the Medical Center parking garage. Changing into fresh clothes, I turned off the stereo and rushed out into the early evening. Only the scent of magnolias in bloom would have improved the air I breathed as I started my truck.

I drove through the Medical Center's parking garage, all four double-helix layers, without seeing Dewey's car. He'd come and gone. Tiny pangs of excitement had my left foot dancing on the floorboard as I drove to the Woodside Racquet Club, where Dewey was to have locked up the car and be inside waiting. I hummed along with the Beach Boys on the radio. I wanted to floor the gas pedal, but too much was at stake to start acting stupid.

Dewey wasn't there.

Neither was his sister's white '72 Impala four-door.

Nor was the money. My money.

Circling aimlessly in the parking lot, I couldn't think. I couldn't react. Dewey had taken off with the money. I'd been had. I knew it in the soft marrow and in the hard edges of my thirty-year-old bones.

From one moment to the next I'd gone from the top of the world to the brittle and utter loss of power. Tailspin. Dive. Crash and burn. I felt dead was what I felt.

I drove to a nearby convenience store, where I looked up Dewey's sister in the phone book. Her name was Della. She lived on Tomahawk Street on the Kansas side. My hands shook as I fisted through the endless series of gear changes on the way to her house. I was dead, but I was doing something about it.

Della met me at the door, holding a silent two-year-old in her arm. She wore ragged cutoffs and a sleeveless T-shirt. She also wore one breast hanging out. The two-year-old stopped nursing to give me the once-over through the screen door.

"I'm looking for Dewey," I said, as casually as my cartwheeling emotions would allow.

"He's gone for a couple days," she said. I raised my eyebrows. It wasn't a last-minute decision on Dewey's part to abort our contract. He'd laid the groundwork. "Dewey owe you money or something?"

"We're friends," I told her. "He was going to help me with a job tomorrow and I just wanted to go over it with him."

"Not tomorrow. His college fraternity all went on a three-day camp-out in the Ozarks. He borrowed my car, left yesterday. Supposed to be back late Saturday."

Dewey had sensed a weakness and worked out his own angle.

"Oh, yeah," I said, snapping my fingers, faking it. "Dewey said he was going down to Arkansas where his uncle's place is."

Della laughed. I wondered if the milk in her breast bubbled.

"Naw," she said. "Uncle Lamar lives in Hot Springs. They weren't going that far."

The hell he wasn't, I thought. The bastard was going to try to clean the money at the track. But he'd have trouble doing that. It was June and the Oaklawn season at Hot Springs ended in April.

"You got nothing to do for a while," Della was saying, "you could come in and have a beer if you want one."

"Another time," I said, perhaps too sharply. She hefted her child on her hip. Her nipple popped from his mouth. It was wet and shiny. I didn't envy the kid.

And I didn't envy Dewey Boone when I caught up
with him.

I was afraid to drive my truck. The whole damn
thing was hexed and I ridiculously thought they had
me pegged. I didn't even know who they might be,
but *they* had my name and number. *They* knew where
to look. Paranoia was taking over. I believed it entirely
possible and somewhat probable that Dewey had
phoned in and told them I was their man.

I wanted a gun and another car to drive. I knew of
one sure place to pick up a gun in a hurry, a gun that
wasn't tied to me by a number, a gun that was loaded.

Police officers across the country were required to
carry off-duty weapons. Those not required to probably did anyway. Usually an officer's off-duty weapon
was smaller and lighter than the service revolver
clipped to his or her black leather belt. They fit a
shoulder holster or slipped easily and snugly into a
purse. Almost always they were short-barreled .38's,
and almost always they fit into a glove compartment.

A strange phenomenon in Merriam, Kansas, one
of the suburbs, had caught my attention. The Merriam
police and fire departments were located across a four-
lane from a huge K mart. Public parking for these city
offices was in front of the recently remodeled brick
building. The help, however, parked out back. The lot
was well lighted, but not a single window of the brick
building looked out upon the cars parked there. The
cars that belonged to the firemen and the cops.

Driving around the area, I discovered an apartment complex just south of the K mart. I left my
brown pickup there in a visitor's parking slot, one
more vehicle belonging to friends or relatives spending a day or two visiting. No one would report it to the
police.

I took off my shirt and tried to blend in with the
suburban surroundings by jogging north. I was thankful I'd chosen tennis shoes for the day's work. The sun
had fully set and I allowed the last light to die further

by jogging six blocks beyond the Merriam fire and police departments.

I wasn't an athlete, but the energy was there. I could have run to Hot Springs, Arkansas, and not felt winded. I would have run to the edge of the continent to strangle that punk. I couldn't have told you honestly whether I planned to use the gun for more than intimidation. I believed, though, that a gun was necessary.

Approaching the lot from behind the civic building, I slowed to a walk. Firemen and cops had about the same taste in cars. How many I broke into before I found a loaded gun was up to luck. Firemen probably stashed off-duty extinguishers instead of weapons.

I started with pickups, just on the chance some gung-ho cop went to the trouble of locking his weapon in the trunk. I was inside a four-wheel-drive monster with a *Police Officers Don't Cop Out* bumper sticker in a wink. Popping open the glove compartment, I wrapped my gloved hand around a snub-nose .38 in a snap-on holster. Even in the dim light I could see the glinting brass edges of one or two rounds in the revolver.

Carrying the gun was like carrying an extra pair of balls. I felt big. I felt my power returning. I ripped off a silver Mazda RX7, a clever little sports car, that was parked to the side of the K mart. The gas tank was full; I was having all the luck.

Three hours later I was driving through Joplin, Missouri, 165 miles south of Kansas City. It was only a few more miles to the Arkansas border. I decided to take the Mazda across state lines, against my usual judgment. What the hell? I had a gun, didn't I? I was on a half-million-dollar mission. Who was going to stop me?

At a truck stop in Bentonville, Arkansas, I pumped my own gas. I bought donuts and cheese curls. I picked up a pint of Johnnie Walker Black and a six-pack of diet Cokes. A package of gum. It was a little after midnight. Between me and Hot Springs was the

Ozarks National Forest *and* the Ouachita Mountains National Forest.

Between me and Dewey Boone were some of the steepest, darkest hairpin turns in these United States. The view was fantastic when the sun was up. The drive was a Grand Prix of speed and steering control. Taking a curve marked twenty-miles-per-hour at thirty was a monumental accomplishment at night. Passing a grinding tractor-trailer rig was playing the odds against death.

I'd be in Hot Springs before the sun got there was my bet.

Chapter 9

Summer was in full bloom in Arkansas and the windshield of the silver sports car was plastered with a variety of bugs. I drove along the row of white turn-of-the-century bathhouses that formed the elongated heart of Hot Springs. The center of the town itself was a national park, the natural spring water belonging to the public. The bathhouses, though, looked as if they belonged to the dead. They looked like mausoleums.

Bathhouse Row was further decorated by a long line of magnificent magnolias. The lawns, expertly manicured, were a softer green and displayed occasional statuary and frequent blossoming shrubs.

I checked my watch. The sun was just now up, but you couldn't tell it by looking. The sky was a humid haze.

I caught a few bars of a mockingbird's song as I drove by the Arlington. On down the avenue was the Majestic. Both were grand hotels, complete with art deco furnishings and hot-spring baths in the base-

ments. A fountain I'd forgotten about appeared like a
ghost bringing rain to the middle of the street. I'd
taken it easy on the Johnnie Walker, allowing myself a
throatful every forty-five minutes. It paced the drive.

The buildings changed into houses seemingly
erected during the War Between the States or soon
after, situated far back from the street on high rises of
poorly tended ground. Small motels and donut shops
stood like squatters to the left and the right, dreams
left over from the fifties. No one, it appeared, had
gotten rich quick.

Soon enough a 7-Eleven was upon me and I
wheeled the silver RX7 into the parking lot. Inside, I
borrowed the local phone book and found a listing for
Lamar Boone. I bought a cup of coffee and asked the
young man at the counter how to get to 1411 McKey.

"A bit in the country," he said. "You need cigarettes or gum? How 'bout a fresh pastry?"

"Just coffee. Which way 'in the country a bit'?"

"End of Central. McKey runs north and south sort
of. You turn south, let's see, that's right if you just go on
down the street. This is Central here in front. Yeah,
fourteen eleven would be south. Numbers should be
on the mailbox. That's seventy-eight cents."

I put a dollar on the counter. He rang up my
coffee.

"I'm trying to remember if the odd numbers are
on the left or the right on the south end," he continued.

"I'll let you know," I said, walking out, leaving
him to pocket my twenty-two cents in change. Information came cheap in Arkansas.

McKey was paved for only two blocks south of
Central. The Mazda bounced and rattled and
squeaked as I drove onto the broken-rock road that
was my rainbow, at the end of which waited a four-
hundred-thousand-dollar pot of gold. And a rusty
Chevy Impala. The odd numbers were on the right. I
pulled over at a black mailbox on a post. In white
letters was painted the name *L. Boone*. There were no

numbers, though, and you couldn't see the house from the road.

Large yards are a southern tradition very much alive in Hot Springs. I couldn't lock up the car because I didn't have a key. I separated two twisted wires and shut off the engine. I stuck the police revolver into the top of the back of my jeans and hiked among the wet weeds that lined a muddy drive between scraggly trees and misshapen bushes. A dog yelped in the far distance to let me know it had begun to rain.

The house, when I finally reached it, was asleep. Dead quiet.

An old Ford pickup was parked out front. An empty rocking chair sat next to a bench swing on the front porch. The drizzling rain drifted into opened windows that looked blankly out at me. I made my way around to the back.

Della's Chevy was parked two steps from the back door of Lamar Boone's house. I looked under the front seat. I pulled out the backseat and tried to see into the trunk. Opening the glove compartment, I found all kinds of junk, including a large screwdriver with a broken plastic handle.

The money was either in the trunk or in the house. I slipped out into the fog-drizzle rain and searched for a rock the correct size and weight. Rocks were everywhere in Arkansas. I placed the tip of the screwdriver angled on the top edge of the lock of the Impala's trunk. I lifted the rock and brought it down on the broken handle of the screwdriver. I felt like a savage, using the rock. I felt like the reason people put up fences.

But the lock popped and the trunk lid lifted. I left the rock and screwdriver where they fell. Inside the trunk were a pair of women's shoes, a bicycle seat, a flattened spare, a loose tire tool. Empty beer cans. A moldy blanket. And two bricks. No jack. No canvas bank bags, no neat bundles of crisp hundred-dollar bills. My money was inside the house.

And it was *my* money. Dewey had forfeited his

share by running off. I remembered that the wet grass in Arkansas in the summer was infested with ticks and often fleas. I hurried onto the small concrete stoop and found the back door to Lamar's house unlocked. My hair was soaked, plastered to my forehead.

Holding the revolver in my right hand, I stepped in out of the rain. I closed the door behind me as quietly as I could and locked it. I stood in the kitchen, noticing that there were dirty dishes in the sink. The wooden floor creaked beneath my steps as I made my way out of the room, convinced that Dewey Boone and his uncle were still in bed.

Inside a small living room with three opened windows, the first thing I noticed was that the television was on with the sound turned off. *Good Morning America.* I stood on a braided rug, stood in my wet jogging shoes, and listened to a pendulum cuckoo clock *click-clack* the passage of time.

I scanned the room, the furniture. No canvas bags. No hundred-dollar bills. I crossed the room and pushed open a door that led into a large bedroom off the front room. One step inside, I froze in place. Summer was over. It was twenty below zero in my bones.

I stopped breathing. The two people on the bed sat up against the iron rails of the headboard, their heads seemingly held in place by nails. I forced myself to breathe in deeply against the inner chill as details slammed into my consciousness. Two windows overlooking the front porch brought in enough gray daylight for me not to be mistaken.

Dewey and Lamar Boone were tied in place; white cords around their necks held their heads up. I remembered that my mother had had a fondness for railed headboards. I stepped closer to be sure, but I already knew too well they both were dead. Each had been shot in the head point-blank. There were two small splatters of blood on the wall.

Someone turned up the volume on the cuckoo clock. It pounded at my temples, the senseless and relentless rhythm of a wooden heartbeat.

Lamar's eyes were closed and his face was badly bruised. From eye to chin, the right side of his face was covered with blood. His mouth was open as if to speak. Blood soaked his bare chest, the sheets. Dewey's dark blue eyes stared at me. It appeared that, like his uncle, Dewey had been shot in the ear. It didn't look as if it had hurt. The expression on Dewey's face wasn't pain.

It was fear. Dewey Boone was too damn young to have had this happen to him. My mind raced to find and cling to a way this might have happened. But only Dewey knew what had gone wrong. Only Dewey knew the mistake he'd made. And Dewey wasn't talking.

Like his uncle, Dewey was shirtless, and as with his uncle, ample blood had stained his neck and chest. I was thankful his executioner had used regular lead rather than hollow tips. Since half of their heads had not been blown away by the exit of the bullets, I guessed a small-caliber weapon had been used. Something no larger than a .32.

Dewey's arms were tied in front at the elbow. A pool of blood coagulated in his navel. I wanted to stop looking but I couldn't. I wanted the cuckoo clock to stop hammering away at me with its screaming noise but it wouldn't. I wondered who had my money now.

I didn't look forward to searching the house, but it would have to be done. I had to know it wasn't there by some fluke. It was possible, after all, that Lamar and Dewey had been executed out of frustration. It was also possible they had been killed for a reason other than the hundreds of thousands of dollars Dewey had helped me steal the day before. But I doubted it. I rubbed my face, suddenly aware that I was physically very tired and emotionally exhausted.

I turned to leave the bedroom, reminding myself not to touch anything, not to leave a single fingerprint. I wanted to run. I looked back and thought I saw Dewey wave his hand at me. A chill ran up my spine, tickling the small hairs on the back of my neck.

How had I missed it? I stared hard to freeze his

hand in place, to put an end to the mirage of Dewey Boone waving bye-bye.

Yet that's exactly what it looked like. His right hand was lifted, his arm a perfect ninety-degree angle from where it was tied at the elbow, locked in space, locked in time. Yesterday's mail.

Dewey had tucked his thumb in against the palm of his hand, leaving four fingers held up in the dim light of the bedroom. His hand looked like the broken wing of a blackbird frozen on the snow. Four, I recalled, was Dewey's lucky number. I couldn't shake the deep-gut feeling that Dewey had meant this wave for me. The cuckoo clock chimed the half-hour.

Chapter 10

Coming back into Lamar Boone's rainy-morning living room, I immediately saw the man sitting in a chair, facing me. A siren sounded in my head. I wondered if he'd been there the entire time, if I'd walked past him on my way in. Impossible, I decided. The man pointing a small gun in my direction, holding it almost comfortably, had come into the living room while I'd stood in the bedroom. He'd sat down and waited.

"Put down the revolver," he said. His voice was gravel.

The idiot clock mocked my own thudding heart as I let the .38 slip from my hand and fall to the rug on the wooden floor of Lamar Boone's living room early on a Friday morning in Arkansas. He motioned with his head and his gleaming pistol toward the couch, where I cautiously moved to sit down.

His hair was silver and modishly cut. He wore a

neatly trimmed mustache that looked almost military in its precision. His face was tan, but wrinkled. The man with the gun wore an expensive white shirt, open at the collar, under a light-blue sports jacket. His slacks were gray. What gave him away were his shoes. They were round-toe, patent leather, high-gloss black. The man was a cop.

We listened to each other breathe as I, sitting across from him, tried to discern the minute shape of a lapel pin he was wearing. It took me a moment to be certain. The design of his lapel pin was a pair of hand-cuffs.

His clothes were too expensive for him to be a regular robbery detective. I couldn't figure it out. A federal agent or even an undercover detective would never have worn a piece of handcuffs jewelry. Neither would a private dick. It was the kind of thing you expected to see on a small-town chief of police at the annual convention in Atlantic City.

"I'm so tired I could be run over by a parked car," he finally said. I didn't laugh. Instead, I studied the gun in his hand, wondering if it was the weapon used to fire bullets into the heads of Dewey and Lamar Boone. The silver-haired stranger noticed the attention I gave his gun and took it upon himself to introduce us.

"Colt thirty-two," he said offhandedly. "Auto-matic. Looks like a toy, but it fits in a pocket and gets the job done. As well as that bulky thirty-eight you just dropped on the floor. Stolen, isn't it? But then you make your living stealing things, don't you, Mr. Frank-lin?"

I didn't say a word.

"Or should I call you Rooster?"

The blue light of the television set cast a depress-ing glow in the corner. Outside, the sun battled the rain clouds . . . and lost. A sudden shower sounded like leaves falling ten times too fast.

"Ray Sargent," he said, after a pause to listen to the rain. I was at a total loss. "St. Louis," he added.

"That's where I have my shop. You ever been in the arch?"

I looked up from Lamar Boone's coffee table. Ray Sargent's face was little more than a mask. The man could have been playing poker for the mortgage on his house. Or sitting in the first pew at Sunday services. The only thing his face told me was his age.

Ray Sargent had been around. He was a reasonably attractive sixty-year-old who looked like a retired Texas Ranger from one of the movies I loved as a kid. Ray Sargent had the patience of poison in a bottle.

"Well, Ray Sargent of St. Louis," I said, wanting to get to the bottom of this before I sweat through my shirt, "you'd be doing me a favor if you let me call the police. Seems a friend of mine and his uncle have been shot."

He laughed. Creek water over gravel, sharp stones.

"Don't," he protested sternly. He patted his chest with his free hand. "Don't make me laugh. Bad heart. Can't take the excitement."

I wondered whom I was trying to kid. The man already knew my name. It would be just like life if this retired asshole cop were an enforcer for the syndicate. St. Louis was an ugly town.

"Three people can keep a secret when two of them are dead," he recited, making his own joke, motioning with his gun toward the door of the bedroom. "You know who said that? Benjamin Franklin, I believe. You related?"

He paused, knowing I wasn't about to say a word.

"Trouble is your accomplice wasn't dead soon enough."

"You didn't kill him then?" It was worth a shot.

"Hoods," Ray Sargent proclaimed. "At least, that's my guess. Kansas City hoods with connections. They beat us both here. Or maybe they even got here before Dewey did. Maybe they knew he was coming this way before either one of us figured it out. They could have been waiting. You catching on yet, Mr. Franklin?"

Yeah, I was catching on. What he was telling me was that Dewey had talked. That he had talked *before* the robbery. What he wasn't telling me was who the hell he was and where the hell my money might be.

"What's amazing is that you didn't. You're pretty good, Franklin. Too bad he wasn't." The older man motioned toward the bedroom door again.

"Good," he repeated. "But I'm better. Guess you could say I've been around that block. Take, for example, that I didn't leave my car parked in the middle of the road. Take, for example, that I'm holding the gun and you're not."

He tried to smile.

"Let me level with you, Rooster. I'm not going to shoot you unless you do something stupid. I just want to talk. I'm getting on in years and I don't like playing Mickey Mouse with thieves. I believe in being, how do they say it these days, 'up front'?"

There was a faded tattoo on the back of his hand. It looked as if it had been an anchor once. Ray Sargent had been in the navy. Judging from his age, probably World War II. Probably the Pacific. This knowledge didn't help me much.

"What do they call you now that you're out?"

I shrugged.

"Still 'Rooster'? They still call you Rooster around the cop shop. It's on your record, you know? Everything you've been called. All your names. It's quite a list."

I raised my eyebrows. My hair was drying to my forehead. I pushed it away with my hand and watched Ray Sargent's gun follow the gesture as a tennis spectator's face follows the movement of the ball from one half of the court to the other.

"Hell," he said, "I know more about you than you do."

The old guy didn't need any encouragement on my part to continue.

"Brown on brown, six foot, one hundred seventy pounds, rooster tattoo on your left breast, two root canals. Father unknown. Mother deceased. Married twice. Daughter from first marriage, whereabouts unknown . . . by you, that is."

I clinched my fists.

"Sure, I know where she lives. I could give you her mom's phone number off the top of my head. See, I didn't have much to do on the plane down here, so I read your paperwork. There's more, but you get the picture."

"FBI?" I asked, angered but determined not to let it show.

Ray Sargent laughed.

"I told you not to do that," he sputtered. "Not to make me laugh. But they wish, son, they fuckin' wish. It'd take the FBI two years and a dozen paid informants to figure this one out.

"However, they're coming in on it. They like the big numbers, the big bucks. It looks good on their year-end stats. They also got this thing about bank robbers. Goes all the way back to Mr. Hoover."

"And you?" I asked. "You got 'this thing' about bank robbers or did you fly down here for the baths?"

The old man chuckled.

"I told you, Rooster," he warned me again about making him laugh.

I'd have liked the guy much more if I'd been the one holding the gun. If I'd known more about him and he'd known less about me.

"But you're right," he said. "I got this thing about bank robbers, too. You might say it's my business. I'm what you call a consultant. You know, an expert. You know what an expert is, don't you, Rooster? An expert is anyone from out of town."

He waited. I listened to the clock and the rain.

"I'm from out of town. I'm a security expert. Top of the line."

"Retired cop?"

"Exactly. Only now I make money. I fly all over

the country to analyze existing security measures and then make a report that includes my recommendations. I call it a five-year plan. Bunch of horseshit, but they like it. It gives 'em goals and it keeps the insurance companies happy."

"And the feds."

"Feds are never happy," Ray Sargent allowed. "Anyway, my most recent client, you're going to love this, was none other than Heartland Savings and Loan."

I didn't say a word. I didn't blink an eye.

"You understand, Rooster? Heartland Savings and Loan. It's a big job. I was spending a day at each of their branches in the Kansas City area. You know, flirting with the girls, getting them to talk. Making the managers nervous, that kind of thing."

I almost smiled. But it wasn't funny. Dewey was murdered and nothing was funny.

"Well, wouldn't you know it, son, I was at the branch on Nall and Sixty-third yesterday. Just standing around chewing a piece of gum and looking like an expert."

"You're after the commission, is that it?" I broke in. "You get twenty percent or something?"

He ignored my question.

"And this Oleta Pryor takes the week's worth to the main office. That's the way they do it, don't ask me. Whoever the Veep likes just drives it over in her car. Supposed to be low-key, something nobody would notice. But you noticed. Alton Benjamin Franklin noticed, yes, sir. But I'm jumping ahead of myself."

Ray Sargent looked at his gun as if to dislodge his memory.

"So anyway, I tag along. Couple of blocks back. And I watch this big green Pontiac run our little lady off the road. Bam, just like that! Now that catches my eye, Rooster. You see, I'm an expert.

"Then I see this guy come running down this hill with a gunnysack. Something out of 'Ma and Pa Kettle Meet Eliot Ness'; right out of the thirties, I'm telling you. And I watch him go running back up the hill with the bank's money. A whole damn lot of the bank's money."

Ray Sargent changed hands, never letting the barrel of his Colt .32 point anywhere but at me. The guy was an expert, all right.

"Four bags full," he continued. "So what am I going to do? Hey, Rooster, I could have chased you. But I *saw* the money go over the hill. You, I didn't care about."

I shot a glance at the stolen police officer's revolver on the rug. Ray followed my gaze with his but kept on talking.

"I had to floor that rental and get around a couple blocks of grandmas driving to the grocery store, but I made it to the other side of the hill in time. Your friend here was pretty slow about things. Must have stopped to have a cigarette or something . . . or maybe he had to relieve himself in the trees. You know, we had this guy in St. Louis had to stop and take a dump every time he held up a store. Left quite a trail, son. Quite a trail.

"Well, I got around there in time to see him driving off. And I fell in behind your friend in traffic. Not for long, you know. I didn't want him to think he was being followed. But I made the plates and let him go."

Suddenly I was tired *and* hungry. I had a throbbing headache. I thought of an apple, a big, red, sweet apple. I thought of how good eating a juicy apple would be. Maybe I'd also nibble on a piece of cheese. I also wondered what might have slowed Dewey down. Surely he didn't stop to count the money.

"Anyway, I gave 'em a description of *your* car. Stolen, right? And they're so damn convinced it got away with the money, the police didn't even comb the area for evidence. They did make up that stuff about the van, though. Just to throw you off.

"You see, Rooster, I'm just a consultant. I didn't want to follow your friend all the way home just to get shot by . . . by somebody like the boys who were here a little earlier."

I creased my brow and the ache moved to the front of my head.

"You wondering why Dewey's sister didn't say nothing about it?"

Once again I shrugged. I was no longer concerned about the details of Ray Sargent's little seek-and-find. I was trying to decide where my money was and what his angle was in all this.

"Paid her, son. Paid her some money. Even told her you might be coming by. Or somebody like you. I was the one who made up that fraternity party. But I guess you paid her, too, huh?"

I let him think what he wanted to think. And I waited for him to tell me something I wanted to know.

"Or maybe you were hosing this girl, who knows?"

"So what's the deal?" I finally asked. "What do you want with me? Pal, if you're after the commission, you have to come up with the money. And mister, I ain't got it."

Ray Sargent crackled with brief laughter. My tough-guy approach must have lacked polish. The gun, however, didn't waver.

"I don't want no commission, Rooster. Shit, no, I don't want no commission."

I finally caught on. Ray Sargent was a vulture waiting for the kill to happen. He was swooping down on his own two wings to carry off my rabbit. This old guy was out to pick up a belated retirement fund.

"So I got a couple hoods and the FBI and now I've got you," I said. "You're after my money, too." My headache eased. He wasn't going to shoot me.

Ray Sargent stood up. He walked over to the revolver on the rug and kicked it across the floor. The loaded weapon ended up in the kitchen. Then the well-dressed older man walked to the front door. He opened it and stood on the threshold. I turned to stare at his figure framed in the doorway.

I watched as he slipped the small automatic into the pocket of his jacket. He smiled and offered a half-hearted salute.

"That's about the size of it," he said. "Only I'm the one going to be getting it. See you around."

And with that he walked out the door, leaving me with my headache and the noise of the clock. Unless the man was struck by lightning as he crossed the yard, I was fairly certain I would indeed be seeing him around.

Chapter 11

I sat on Lamar Boone's couch and stared at the soundless television. Local programming was on, the morning reruns. I watched an aging Theodore Cleaver climb into the family car last. He grinned at me as if something were up as Ward backed them out the driveway. A name was at the tip of my thought's tongue.

Dewey Boone had told me that someone special gave him the number four as his lucky number. A fortune-teller? An old aunt? An astrology writer in a horoscope magazine? The chick chimed eight times and the chill rode back up my spine.

I walked into the kitchen and picked up the re-volver I'd stolen in Merriam, Kansas. I used a damp dish towel to wipe my prints off anything I might have touched before discovering the bodies. Then I got the hell out of there.

Ray Sargent had pulled the distributor cable from under the hood of the RX7. He'd taken it with him or had tossed it into the thick undergrowth alongside the road. I was tired and hungry. And wet. I hitchhiked in the rain, wanting a big juicy apple and four sacks of hundred-dollar bills.

Hitchhiking on that Arkansas rock road meant walking. I found my way on foot to the 7-Eleven on Central and phoned for a cab. I bought a box of chocolate-iced donuts and a large fountain drink. I needed all the caffeine and sugar I could get. I'd get me an apple some other time, some other life.

The cab dropped me off at the Majestic Hotel, where an entire fleet of out-of-state cars waited in the parking lot cut out of the rock bluff across the street. I picked out a late-model Buick and was driving into Ft. Smith with the radio on when it came to me in a song about *Rose Marie.*

Thank God for the oldies craze.

That was it. That was the message from Dewey Boone. Four was his lucky number that day at the track and Rose Marie was the woman who'd given it to him. And Rose Marie was the woman he'd sent me to check out. She was the key to the imprint of his four fingers on the gray matter between my ears. Rose Marie . . . No! It was something else.

The radio again. Another oldie. "Return to Sender." Rose Sender. Rose Cinda. Rose Linda. Oh, yeah, that was it! Rosalinda! Yes, yes, yes! *Rosalinda* was the name on Dewey's outstretched fingertips. He'd pointed the way for me.

Damn, I thought, if it wasn't always a woman.

I decided to skip over into Oklahoma to get another car and make my way to Kansas City, where Rosalinda, and no doubt Ray Sargent, would be waiting. Kansas City was where this game would be played out, and it was my move.

Someone had found the bodies by now, I thought. Oklahoma looked good to me on the other side of the river. I wiped off the gun and threw it from the bridge and into the murky water of the Arkansas River as I crossed into another state. My arms were heavy and my hands felt like fingerless clams as I drove north toward Kansas.

I needed a place to rest. Once inside Kansas, that flat state of amber waves of grain, I'd get a room. I'd think this through. I was too exhausted to yawn when the local police turned on the red lights in Madrigal, Oklahoma.

I pulled over. What I should have done was race them to the border and, once inside Kansas, abandon the car.

"What about breakfast?" I asked my Okie jailer. He stood in the open door of my cage, holding a bar of soap in one hand, a once-white towel draped over his arm. In his other hand was a weighted nightstick.

"You're on your way out, Rooster. We had your shirt washed."

"I'd rather have breakfast," I said, taking the towel and the soap. He backed out of the cage and pointed toward the back of the building with his nightstick.

"They're waitin' on you. Wash up."

I walked in my socks to a stool against the back wall. A showerhead stuck out from the wall, even with my breastbone. There was a patterned brass cover over the drain in the floor. It reminded me of waffles. I wanted to eat. I took off my jeans, my socks, my Jockey shorts. Familiar-looking roaches, large and black, came leaping out of the drain as soon as the water touched it. Deputy Dog stared at the wall and fiddled with the nightstick while I scrubbed under a meager spray of warm water.

"What day is it?" I asked, drying my hair with the towel.

"Tuesday, you know that. You only been here since Friday."

"That's like saying I've only been tortured with heated pokers and cattle prods for a *few* hours."

"At least you ain't going to Texas."

A Sequoyah County deputy waited for me in the front office. He was a slight man in his fifties, with a face that was slightly too narrow to ever express full-fledged merriment.

"Am I ever glad to see you," I told him as I put on my clean plaid shirt and stuffed the tail inside my jeans. I was given my belt and my shoes, laces intact. I was slightly embarrassed to be wearing tennis shoes among men in polished boots and gunbelts.

Something was up, I decided, when I checked my wallet and discovered that the more than three hundred dollars that had been there when I'd been arrested was, in fact, still there. They even gave me back my keys. There was an extra set in my glove compartment, in my Datsun pickup parked in a Kansas City suburb.

Someone had pulled a couple strings. The FBI?

I hadn't the slightest notion the jail in Sallisaw, Oklahoma, would be any nicer than the jail in Madrigal. The notion I had was that once charges were filed, I'd have bail set. Simple auto theft. Simple joyride. I hadn't tried to sell the car. Even with my record, you got bail for auto theft if you could convince the judge you'd only stolen the car for transportation and not for profit.

I had enough bail-bond cards to get Chuck Manson a two-week vacation in Honolulu. They weren't all in the same name, but I'd only need one.

"Don't I owe you all something for the food and linen?" I asked the room as the Sequoyah deputy led me by the elbow out the door and to his car parked in front of the station. The deputy from Sallisaw hadn't drawn his gun.

"Take 'er easy, Rooster," my private jailer called as the door closed behind us. The morning sunlight stung my eyes. I blinked repeatedly. My new custodian loaded me into the backseat of a recent model Dodge by placing his hand on the top of my head as I bent over to slip inside. There were no handles on the inside of the back doors. A wire mesh screen separated the front seat from the back. Other than that, it was a fairly standard issue of automobile.

"You got red lights inside the front grill?"

"Yup," the sheriff's deputy said. "Most people go ahead and stop for 'em."

"You had breakfast?"

"Yup."

"How 'bout stopping for coffee somewhere along the way?"

He'd taken off his gun and had laid it on the seat next to him. We drove ten miles over the speed limit down Highway 66. The only radio in the car was a police scanner. It was turned down too low to hear. I reminded myself never to steal a county police car.

Even though I was headed in the opposite direction of Rosalinda, my spirits were up. It felt good to be wearing a shirt. And I had the strange feeling I could walk away any time I wanted to.

We crossed the Lake O'The Cherokees and were heading into Grove, Oklahoma, when I told the deputy driver I had to pee.

"Stop somewhere and grab us some Twinkies and something to drink," I offered. "It's on me."

"Yup," was all he said.

We stopped at a place called Swink's Dairy Inn. You wondered if cows slept there when they went on vacation. The deputy carried his holstered gun in his hand and followed me to the outside entrance to the men's room. He waited outside while I read the graffiti on the condom machine. When he pounded on the door, I opened it and pushed him down with both hands. His holstered gun fell as he fell, and I picked it up.

I made a run for it.

I ran around the outside corner of the building and saw only the county-issue beige Dodge parked there. I jerked open the driver's door and was only mildly surprised to find the keys in the ignition.

As I pulled out of Swink's Dairy Inn and onto Highway 66, I watched the rearview mirror for a glimpse of the deputy coming running around the cinder-block building. He never showed. I hoped he wasn't hurt in the fall, and I suddenly felt sorry for Dewey Boone.

It came over me like a wave. There was no reason a kid that young had to die the way he did. Maybe once I found Rosalinda and my money, I'd look up the thugs who had done in Dewey and his uncle. It was the least I could do. Well, almost. The least I could do at the moment was change cars and get my butt out of Oklahoma.

I found the switch that turned on the flashing red lights behind the grill of the Dodge and floored the accelerator. The thing topped out at eighty-five.

Too easy, I decided. My escape had been too easily accomplished. I was in a 1981 Skylark, driving north toward Baxter Springs, Kansas, only two miles after having crossed the state line, when I got nervous about it. There was a large white house and a huge green field on my left. The house had two-story white columns in front. If I lived in that house, I thought, I wouldn't be up to these kinds of things.

I blamed my uneasiness on Ray Sargent, the mysterious security consultant from St. Louis. I blamed it on the murders of Dewey and Lamar Boone. I blamed my anxiety on the FBI and the damn cuckoo clock in Lamar's house.

I'd been set up, I decided. I'd been let go.

Because somebody knew about the Heartland Savings & Loan robbery. It was important to *somebody* that I lead them to the money. More important than my facing charges for having stolen a car in Sallisaw.

Instead of continuing north, I slipped sideways out of Baxter Springs, heading west on Highway 166, hugging the Oklahoma state line almost as closely as the road hugged the soft hills between me and Wichita. If Ray Sargent were right and the hoods who'd killed Dewey and his uncle were connected, I had more than the FBI to worry about.

The Kansas City mob was classic Syndicate. They

skimmed profits from Las Vegas casinos. They organized prostitution and drug trafficking. They had interests in a hundred more or less legitimate companies. They provided collection services for small-time bookies without the bookies having requested the service. And they cheated on their taxes . . . like everybody else. Unlike everybody else, they shot people in the head who got in their way.

They folded the bodies of their competitors into the trunks of cars left abandoned in municipal parking lots.

Chapter 12

It was Tuesday afternoon, sunny and warm. There was only one oasis. My camel and I were on our way to Wichita to lie low while I decided how best to sneak into Kansas City and put my hands on a woman named Rosalinda.

Driving through Augusta, twenty miles outside Wichita, another thought occurred to me. Something had convinced me that Ray Sargent was telling the truth; but what if I was wrong? It was entirely possible that the .32 automatic the old man had held on me was the same gun that had fired bullets into the heads of Dewey and Lamar Boone. It was entirely possible that Ray Sargent was a professional.

The voice of gravel belied a smoothness of character, a control that reminded me of someone who killed for a living. Were Ray Sargent a hit man, I had no business poking around for Rosalinda in Kansas City. I had no business poking around Kansas City, period. But dammit, the money was mine. So what if the perfect crime hadn't been so perfect after all?

And there was a chance that whoever had executed Dewey Boone and his uncle already had my money. But there was an equal chance they had walked away empty-handed. I figured the odds at ten to one in my favor that Rosalinda would provide the answer. Even if my money was already being banked in Rio—and I doubted it—it was something I wanted to know. I *had* to know. Dewey had told me something in death and that something was a woman named Rosalinda.

I'd find her. You say something often enough it makes it come true. I turned off the radio and made up the words to my own sweet song. It was the kind of thing turning thirty made you do. The title of the song was nothing more than a girl's first name.

Carolyn Sakowski and Paul Valley were my best and equal friends. The house on Jeanette Street in Wichita looked like home as I walked across the lawn. I'd left the Skylark parked in front of a bar on North Broadway. The house was a two-story clapboard, painted white, with a covered porch across the front. The key, as always, was on a hook under the edge of the porch, behind three concrete steps that lifted you up to it.

Flannery, Carolyn's golden retriever, barked from inside the fenced backyard. I rang the bell, holding the key in my mouth. I also held my hands up to my face, wrists limp, as if I were a dog begging for food. It always made Carolyn laugh.

I'd met Paul in the McAlester pen. He'd moved to Wichita and picked up a job at the university, sweeping floors while he worked on a degree. Carolyn owned a bookstore. Paul was in the store, looking mostly, killing time, when Carolyn approached and asked if she could help him find something.

"Got any books with pictures of pregnant women with their clothes off?" Paul said. Eventually they hit it off, but it took some time. Paul had to make four or five more visits to the store before she'd even talk to him.

Now, they were about as happy as an ex-con and a
woman ever could be. They were, in a way, my security in a crazy world. And to a fault, I thought of them
as a couple, a single entity.

I rang the bell again.

We remained good friends, the three of us, because I didn't live in the same town. They came to
Kansas City for an occasional ball game. I went to
Wichita to get drunk on somebody's front porch and
talk to the spirits that surrounded us all when we
drank too much. We went on vacations together, usually road trips to racetracks in Louisville or Louisiana,
Florida or New Mexico.

I put the key in the lock and walked in.

At first I didn't understand the shuffling going on.
A man I didn't know stood next to the couch, buttoning his shirt, zipping his pants. Carolyn stood between
him and me, wrapped in a knitted afghan. There was
an unmistakable blush on her cheeks.

"Alton," she cried far too loudly. "What are *you*
doing here?"

For the life of me, I couldn't think of a thing to say.
There was nothing to do with my hands.

"I'd better be going," the man buttoning his shirt
said, waiting for me to move out of the doorway. Carolyn ignored him and pointed toward the kitchen. Like
a good boy I followed her directions and walked stiffly
across the room, around the bar, and out of sight. I
went straight to the fridge and got out two cans of
beer. I opened one and drank it down.

I was starting on the second when she came into
the room. The front door shut with a bang, as if pushed
by a hot wind rushing through an empty house. I
smiled stupidly and shook my head from side to side. I
listened to the sound of a car starting.

"Holy shit," I said.

Carolyn couldn't bring herself to grin. "You get
me one of those?"

I handed her the beer I held. I stared.

"Haven't you ever walked in on someone before?"

"Once," I said. "But I was just a kid."

"Well, now you're not," Carolyn said spritely. "Paul's been gone since early May. I don't know if he's coming back. I don't even know if he's still alive. I kind of thought he might be with you."

Her last sentence was a question she didn't want to ask. I shook my head no. I hadn't seen him either.

"You know," I finally said, "I kind of always thought it would be me. I mean, if you ever got around to this sort of thing."

"You know," Carolyn said, "so did I."

She turned and walked out of the kitchen, holding her afghan around her waist. I got another beer from the fridge and waited in the front room while she went upstairs to change. I didn't have to wait long. She came down in her robe, still holding her can of beer.

Carolyn was an angular woman with high cheekbones and long legs. Her hair was always sensibly cut and never quite reached her shoulders. The thing I always thought of when I thought of Carolyn was how she laughed. She laughed with her shoulders and her face. When she laughed standing up you'd swear she was dancing.

I stood when she came into the room and we gave each other a hug. I kept my hands where they belonged.

"You lost weight," she said. "Everything okay?"

"You, too," I said. Women like Carolyn always felt skinny to me. Even the ones who thought they needed to lose twenty pounds. Carolyn released her arms from around me, turned on a lamp, and sat down heavily on the couch. The blinds were drawn. She dropped her feet on the coffee table covered with books and magazines and drank from her beer.

"We could get Mexican or barbecue," she offered. "Let me take a shower and put something on and we'll go out and see how drunk we can get in a state that doesn't allow liquor sold by the drink."

She finished her beer, however, before getting up to change. I sat on the front porch, wondering what it would take to get Carolyn to laugh at a time like this, and watched the sun die behind the trees across the street. A bat came out and chased bugs, working what looked like to me a figure eight cut through the dust. Eternity. I figured there'd always be bats and bugs.

Tuesday night in Wichita, Kansas, and maybe Carolyn was right. What I needed was a night in the cowboy bars on North Broadway. The Coyote Club or the Pirate's Cove. Maybe what she needed was someone to listen. I knew that what I wanted was for someone else to talk.

"It had to happen sooner or later," Carolyn was saying as the waitress brought us our second pitcher of beer. "Anybody worthwhile never sticks around. They know enough to walk away *before* things get boring."

I didn't have the heart to argue. I knew Paul was a lot like me. And I knew if I were involved with a woman as wonderful as Carolyn, I wouldn't take off unless I took off for good.

"You guys think you're cowboys or what?"

"Maybe," I said seriously. "Maybe that's it."

Carolyn looked more beautiful than ever. She was older than me by five or six years at least, but you'd never guess it. You had to look close to locate the one or two lines at the corners of her eyes, around the edges of her mouth. The word *paunch* couldn't find a place to land on Carolyn's body.

"What's he after, Alton? Another life? Why can't one life be enough?"

I didn't have any answers.

"Are we going to sleep together tonight?"

"I doubt it," I said.

"So do I."

I wanted to say that I was sorry about her and Paul. I just shook my head. There was a reason Carolyn and I would not be sleeping together. It would ruin everything for both of us if we did. I counted on

Carolyn's being Carolyn, and I wouldn't risk throwing that away. Not yet, anyway. And neither would she.

I told her about the girl in the yellow dress.

We ended up in a place where they kept the lights off. We danced. We stayed beyond last call, talking the bartender into letting us have a six-pack to go. Carolyn drove us home in her Subaru, repeatedly making the wrong gear decision when it came time to shift.

She surprised me by camping out in the wicker rocker on her front porch once we were home.

I sat beside her on the painted boards of the porch itself. We sipped our warm beers. A few stars held still over the treetops. They were watching us.

"I'm going to fall in love," I blurted out.

"Why?" she said. "You never love anything for long that you're allowed to keep." Did she mean me or Paul?

"I don't know why, but I am."

More than a few moments went by. One or two of the stars got up to go to the bathroom. The grass and the bushes and sidewalk slept.

"Alton," Carolyn said in a new voice, a little girl's voice. "Is it all right if I cry?"

"It might be good for both of us if you do."

The night shadows looked like camels to me, camels sitting down on folded legs. I could even hear the noise that sleeping camels and quietly weeping women make. And I could hear the sound of my heart break. More than almost anything, I wanted Carolyn and Paul to last forever.

Later, Carolyn stood up from the chair without saying a word, scattering stars and camels. She went inside to go to sleep. We both knew I'd be gone in the morning. I'd been lucky enough to get what I'd come by for: the strength to carry on, the strength to return to Kansas City and see this thing through.

Chapter 13

It was just before six in the morning when I rolled off the couch and made my way into the bathroom to clean up. I felt incredibly good, considering the amount of sleep and beer I'd had the night before. To shave, I used one of Carolyn's disposable razors. Then I showered, careful not to sing.

Downstairs I made coffee. I rinsed out my socks in the kitchen sink and tossed them in the dryer. Looking inside the small closet at the foot of the stairs, I discovered that Paul had left a few shirts behind. Knowing he wouldn't mind, I put one on, a bright yellow Hawaiian shirt, patterned with large green leaves and even larger crimson flowers. While my socks tumbled, I sipped a cup of coffee and read the Wednesday morning Wichita *Eagle-Beacon*.

Rosalinda fell in my lap. Reading the agate baseball boxes somehow reminded me of telephone-book listings. Rosalinda, it was clear to me, *was* in the book. All I had to go was get myself to Kansas City and look her up.

After putting on my socks and shoes, I left a short note for Carolyn. Then I set out to find a car to drive to Kansas City in.

It was remarkable, I realized, the number of cars I'd stolen since Thursday, since the green Pontiac crash-car. It was a fact, though, that the police didn't take stolen-car reports all that seriously. Unless you were stopped for a moving violation and they ran your tags through the computer, you were generally off free. Even then, you might be able to convince a particular patrolman that the car belonged to your uncle. If you knew the owner's name. If you had some fake keys hanging from the ignition.

It took an average of three days before a tag number was listed on the state's computer as flat-out stolen. A kid wasn't considered a runaway, for instance, until it was too late to find him. Insurance adjusters were by far better at locating stolen cars than the police, much as private detectives specialized in missing persons.

The nice thing about insurance adjusters was that they didn't pull you over on the highway. They didn't find the car you'd stolen until it had been abandoned.

There was an '84 Thunderbird automatic parked on a side street that caught my eye. A huge hedge hid the car from the windows of the house it was parked nearest to. Once inside the 'bird, I discovered the car was loaded. Full power, tilt wheel, air and cruise control. There was also a quality am/fm stereo setup. The luxury interior included fake-velvet upholstery, power seats, and power windows. I filled it with unleaded premium at a Koch station just outside Wichita on Highway 54.

Between Wichita and Emporia, Kansas, lie the Flint Hills. And you can see miles and miles of rolling, natural grassland. Nothing but a crossing train keeps you from driving eighty. I stopped to use the restroom at the Matfield Green Howard Johnson's on I-35. A small bronze plaque had been erected in memory of Knute Rockne. His plane, according to the plaque, had gone down near here.

Knute couldn't have picked a better place to die.

Even from inside a coffin, the Kansas landscape provided total freedom from the feeling of claustrophobia. Your thoughts, even in death, were afforded room to breathe. The football field reached in all directions forever.

Paul Simon complained on the radio about his little town as I parked the Thunderbird in the visitor's slot next to my brown Datsun pickup at the apartment complex behind the K mart in Merriam, Kansas. It was noon when I tugged the twisted wires apart and let the radio go off, the engine die.

The best approach was the direct approach.

Weary of playing cops and robbers, I drove straight to
my apartment. If Ray Sargent had paid someone to sit
outside my apartment building, so be it. If the CIA was
hiding behind my shower curtain, so be it. It was important to me to read the phone book, to make a call or
to take a drive, whichever seemed the more expedient
way to contact Rosalinda.

Driving along Forty-third Street, toward Thompson, I changed my mind. Instead of parking at my
building, I cut over to Booth and drove into the hous-
ing projects three blocks north of my apartment complex. I hopped out of my pickup as if I belonged there,
trying not to make it apparent I was locking the door,
and marched with concentrated purpose up the street
toward home.

It might have been my acting talent or it might
have been Paul's shirt, but nobody said a word to me
and nobody stopped talking as I strode by. The hous-
ing projects were not a nice neighborhood. The resi-
dents were rumored to be of the sort who'd kill their
next of kin for the amount of money I had in my
wallet. And they looked the part.

To tell the truth, I felt charmed.

I was protected by Rosalinda's magic and the aura
of a man about to self-actualize. I couldn't have been
more nervous. I couldn't have felt more rushed. There
was electricity at the tips of my fingers. And I couldn't
have been happier. I clambered up a brushy hill, over
a chain-link fence that separated the apartments' tennis court from the projects.

The back door to my building, the so-called security door, was propped open with a rock.

Inside my apartment, everything was the same
except for a bit more dust. I grabbed a beer out of the
fridge and set about finding the phone book, which
turned up under the edge of my bed.

There was no Rosalinda in the white pages, at
least not as a last name. It might take me a few hours to
search through the first names. It might take me just
this side of an eternity if I called every initial *R* used in

place of a first name. But I was confident. I held her for the first time in my hands. Rosalinda was in the book.

As a lark, I checked the business pages at the back of the book and was only mildly surprised to find Rosalinda there. Of course she'd been waiting for me. Of course she was listed simply as Rosalinda. Of course there was an address and a phone number. Rosalinda was listed as a fortune-teller in the 800 block of Garfield. It was a Kansas-side exchange. I decided to drive rather than call.

As if to mock my endeavor, the phone rang. For an instant I thought it was Rosalinda calling me. I decided not to answer it.

It stopped ringing. For a minute. Then started ringing again.

It wasn't Wynona. She'd have given up letting the phone ring a couple of days back. It wasn't unlikely that she might call now and then to see if I'd come home, but she wouldn't have called the number twice. Neither would Ray Sargent. People anticipated your answering the phone when you're home. No answer, in their minds, meant I wasn't there yet. Someone who knew me better knew I might just need convincing. It wasn't rare for me to answer the phone after fifteen or twenty rings.

I walked into the bedroom and picked up the blasted thing.

"What?" I said in a voice I hoped was deeper than my own.

"Alton," Carolyn sighed, relieved. "Are you all right?"

"Fine," I told her and then, more cheerfully, "what's up?"

"Efrem Zimbalist, Jr."

"Huh?"

"No kidding, Alton. The F-B-I. This honest-to-God FBI agent came by the bookstore this morning."

"Yeah?"

"And asked me if I knew you."

"Yeah."

"Well, I told him that I did. I didn't think I could lie about that. They'd know that much, wouldn't they, to be talking to me in the first place?"

My escape *had* been set up. They'd followed me, or at the least they'd figured out I was headed for Wichita yesterday. Somebody was on to me. Somebody had called the FBI or the FBI knew a lot more about the Heartland Savings & Loan robbery than I'd suspected. Like the rest of Americans my age, I was a victim of television propaganda and thereby scared shitless of the FBI. J. Edgar Hoover lived in the sinking heart of me.

"And he wanted to know if I'd heard from you."

"Carolyn, what'd you tell him?"

"I told him you were a friend of Paul's and that the two of you had taken off together."

"Carolyn! That's great."

Only the FBI knew better. Maybe.

"I told him I'd received a postcard from some town in Oregon and he wanted to see it. I told him I was pretty pissed off at Paul and had thrown the thing away. He asked if I could remember the name of the town. I tried to remember, I told him, but it wouldn't come to me. Then I told him it might have been a truck stop and not a town anyway."

"Then what'd he say?"

"He asked if I'd ever seen your tattoo and if I'd ever heard anyone call you Rooster. I said, 'You mean the tattoo on his ass?'"

Carolyn laughed. I could picture her shoulders shaking. As she laughed, something new occurred to me.

"Carolyn," I said in a hushed whisper of urgency. "You think they still bug phones, the FBI?"

We were both suddenly and very quiet for the longest time. In her silence I could hear Carolyn's masked desire to ask me what kind of trouble I was in.

"It doesn't matter," I finally said. "I'm due at the airport in less than an hour and it's bye-bye to this ol' town."

She waited for me to continue. I didn't. I was listening to a government car starting up inside my brain, two guys in dull suits on their way to K.C. International in an effort to head me off at the pass.

"Alton?" Carolyn began.

"*Shhh,* everything's okay." I hung up the phone. Maybe it wasn't bugged. Maybe they'd placed an electronic homing device in my tennis shoe and that's how they knew I'd gone to Wichita. It didn't matter; I was out of jail and on my way soon to meet Rosalinda. And everything *was* going to be okay.

Understandably, I was sleepy. As if preparing for a first date, I decided to wait till darkness to visit Rosalinda. I'd drive by and see what was there. Fortune-tellers in Kansas City work out of their homes as a rule. I took off my clothes and without opening the curtains fell asleep on the bed, hoping to dream a perfect ending to my nice, clean crime gone dirty.

I didn't.

When I woke up, it was dark and my neck ached. I was hungry and excited. I took a hot shower and scrubbed as if my life depended on my personal hygiene. I brushed my teeth until my wrist ached, then I flossed twice.

There's a piano bench in my bedroom. It looked for the world like a coffee table. On top of it I kept a yellow-and-red-striped serape. Next to my small black-and-white television from Sears, I have stacked three deep wooden drawers from a dilapidated dresser. I used them as bookshelves. They held my paperbacks, mostly books with the word *blood* in the title.

One drawer served as my collector's bookcase. In it, I'd arranged my classics. Those included first-printing, twenty-five-cent Perry Mason and Mike Shayne paperbacks.

Before leaving, I set aside the television. I took away the makeshift bookcases and left them on the carpet. I tossed the serape on the bed. Inside the piano bench that did not look like a piano bench were com-

plete sets of false identification cards, various burglary
tools (including a very expensive set of stainless-steel
lock picks in a leather case), two extra slim-jims, and a
spare ignition ratchet.

There were two boxes of latex surgical gloves. All
told, it was enough to send an ex-convict back to
prison.

There was also a color photograph of my daughter
when she was two months old. More than a dozen
savings account passbooks in her name. A black-and-
white picture of my mother taken when she was sev-
enteen. She'd been elected Yearbook Queen that year.
It was where I got my good looks.

And there were sixteen hundred dollars in cash.
Twenties. Tender love letters from my government's
treasury to me. I pocketed all of it. No telling where
the night might lead.

Only when I was ready to leave, did I look out the
window. A Trans Am was parked in front of my building, a car I'd never seen before. I watched with interest as the passenger's door popped open and a slight
guy in black slacks and a white shirt climbed out. He
leaned against the car, smoking a cigarette, and stared
off into the distance, as if he were looking for something.

As if he were looking for me.

The driver was a heavier man with dark hair. The
racket from the car's stereo blasted tinnily into the
evening that surrounded us. I'd exit my building
the way I'd come in: through the back and over the
chain-link fence. I had better clothes on this time so I'd
have to be careful. There was a woman waiting for me
so I'd be very careful. A small, tough part of me
wanted to go out front and ask the two guys if they'd
been to Arkansas recently.

Chapter 14

My lucky number was just around the corner.

And another corner. The 800 block of Garfield was lined with parked cars by the time I got there. Folks home from work, watching the tube. Most of the cars were recent models in fairly good shape. I circled the block, wondering if the dash of foreign cologne I'd applied at my apartment was too strong. I'd been saving the cologne for a special occasion.

I turned the radio off and drove back by, slowing considerably. A small spotlight illuminated a large plywood sign in a front yard. ROSALINDA was spelled out across the top of the sign in arching letters, in bright red on the whitewashed board. At the bottom of the sign was a phone number. And in between them was the huge figure of a human hand outlined in red paint.

The word *consultant* was written in black letters in the middle of the hand. I thought of Ray Sargent. I thought of having my palm read by Rosalinda, wondering whether she would see herself between the lines of my hand, a hand held out and open, a hand waiting to be fed four hundred thousand in cash.

There was such a gathering of parked cars that I figured she must have been conducting a séance. I pictured a motley group of well-off middle-agers struggling for a glimpse of another world, their eyes closed, holding hands. I straightened my tie as I walked around the short end of the block and onto Garfield Street. Rosalinda's plywood hand seemed to offer a friendly greeting.

I scuffed the toe of one of my new shoes on an empty liquor bottle, sending it rattling into the gutter.

Rosalinda's house was a long Victorian two-story that reminded me of a boarding house. Lights glowed behind pulled blinds in many of the windows. The windows facing the street were topped with horizontal pieces of leaded glasswork. Stone lion heads protected the steps leading to the front door.

It wasn't that I expected a chorus of angels to break into heavenly song when I knocked on the door. But maybe.

Unless angels were wearing red satin garter belts and fishnet hose, unless angels were wearing pirate-black G-strings, unless angels were wearing red-lace underwire demi-bras, unless angels had successfully completed the Mark Eden bust development course since I'd been to Sunday school, it was no angel who answered Rosalinda's front door.

Her hair looked like a wig and she wore more makeup than Boy George. She smiled knowingly and took my hand to bring me inside a small reception room, done up in red lightbulbs screwed into the lamps.

Three couches lined the wall. The soft white carpeting was deep enough to lose your wallet in should you be foolish enough to drop it. Two men, also wearing ties, sat on either end of one couch. One leafed through a recent copy of *Penthouse* magazine. The other avoided eye contact by staring across the room at a window.

"Drinks are on the house," my angel told me. "I'm Bernice."

"I always thought they would be," I said absent-mindedly. "On the house, that is," I added quickly.

There was a large aquarium full of fragile-looking fish. The colorful small life swam in circles to the rhythm of a funky station playing on a console stereo in the corner. It sounded like disco Marvin Gaye.

"Preferences?" Bernice asked, leaning gently into me.

"I'm sorry?" I preferred oldies, actually.

"Cash or charge?"

"I came to have my fortune read."

"Sure you did, honey." Bernice's hand released

mine, slipped around my back, and tested the muscle of my left buttocks. "You aren't connected in any way with any law enforcement agency, are you?"

"No," I said, staring at the fish, "I am not." *This is not a whorehouse,* I repeated to myself. *This is not a whorehouse. This is not a whorehouse. This is not a whorehouse!* Then she squeezed my rear again. This was a whorehouse.

My heart exploded. But I stood up straight like a good soldier, my dream of Rosalinda fragmented into mist, acid rain. Bernice's other hand loosened the knot of my tie. This would have been easier had I been drunk.

"I'm very agile," the angel told me, lifting on the toes of her spike heels to nibble at my ear, to press home her point. If there was one thing I knew about brothels in Kansas City, Kansas, it was who owned them. The same guys who owned Sam Geolas. The same close-knit group who, according to Ray Sargent, were responsible for the bullet in Dewey Boone's youthful head.

It strangely added up. They knew to follow Dewey Boone to Arkansas, because Dewey Boone himself had told them about the robbery. Had told someone. And Dewey had left me one message: *Rosalinda.* His lucky number. A mob-managed whorehouse.

"Is Rosalinda here tonight?" Possibly there was a working girl who went by the name of the business.

"What's wrong with me?"

"No, really," I said impatiently. "Is there a Rosalinda?"

"The only Rosalinda here is the name on the sign out front."

"Number four then," I blurted out. Words in an emergency. Dewey's lucky number. Perhaps it was my own mangled faith that kept me insisting that Rosalinda was a person. Perhaps Dewey had meant that he'd picked up his lucky number at this whorehouse. But the way he'd said it that day at the track had

convinced me Rosalinda was a person. I couldn't let go
of the notion.

"Number four," I repeated. "Carry out."

"Why didn't you say you were a regular?"

My hostess released her hold on me and marched
from the room. Bernice looked good both coming and
going, and the men on the couch knew enough to
glance up when Bernice moved her booties across the
room.

She returned momentarily, a notebook in her
hand. She lifted her eyebrows.

"Rooster," I said. "Rooster Barnsdale." Bernice
rolled her eyes.

"A hundred to the house," was her reply. I
counted out five twenties and handed them to her. I
held another twenty in my palm. When she looked
back up at me, I offered it to her.

"I'm in a hurry," I explained. I winked.

"What rooster ain't, honey? What rooster ain't?"

Bernice tucked the twenty in her G-string and
walked out again. I stood around watching the fish. A
part of me wanted to slip into the tank with them. It
wasn't easy trying to force myself to believe the fact
that Rosalinda was not a person, not a woman, not the
girl of my dreams and the love of my life. I was, to put
it minimally, deflated.

Disconsolate. There was no joy in Mudville. There
was no joy in discovering that Rosalinda was not my
Spanish-eyed mystic beauty. That she was instead the
name of a Gypsy front for a mob cathouse in Kansas
City, Kansas. I'd been looking forward to something
more spiritual.

"Number four" turned out to be a young girl who
called herself Corinne. She looked young enough not
to be alcoholic. She looked young enough to be a tem-
porary pass-through. She looked young enough to talk,
given the opportunity. For the moment we chatted
about things capitalistic. I wanted to flatter her a little.
I wanted her to like me if it were at all possible and
settled on three hundred for the night.

"Put on your riding shoes, Corinne," I said.

She went into another room to get her purse and a light jacket. Corinne returned with Bernice. I was instructed to put my arm around Corinne and to say cheese.

"Now grin real big, honey," Bernice chided, pointing the lens of her Polaroid at me. I stuck out my tongue. The flash went off. "Okay, kids," Bernice said, "the night is young."

Everyone, I thought, was into security these days. If Corinne turned up badly bruised in the morning, or even dead, the boys in the back knew exactly whom they would be looking for. Whatever happened to trust in your fellowman and whoremonger?

Corinne was visibly disappointed in my Datsun pickup. Which was only fair; I was disappointed in Corinne. She smacked her gum.

Corinne was supple, slightly chubby with round, full breasts under a sparsely sequined V-neck sweater. The sweater was pink. The sequins were silver. She wore tight silver-colored shorts over a pair of pink panty hose. Corinne's hair was tightly permed but long. Mousy brown. She probably considered it blond. I didn't. Her eyes were the same dull brown.

Corinne had interesting eyebrows, though, but not four hundred dollars' worth.

Corinne's purse sat between us. She was waiting. She appeared eager. Corinne reminded me of the type of girl who gravitated toward motorcycle gangs. The type of girl who'd decided her place in life was to be used for somebody else's good time. When the other guy laughed, she knew she was having fun.

I drove as if I were going somewhere, but I had nowhere in mind. I came back down Seventh Street to Southwest Boulevard, cut over to Missouri, toward the river quay. I crossed the Broadway Bridge, tossing a quarter in the plastic bucket at the toll booth. The river was a dark mystery of smooth shadows.

Rosalinda was a bust, I concluded. Number four

had fallen on its face and was riding in the truck next to me. I thought of calling the FBI to see if they had any ideas where the money might be. I thought of letting Ray Sargent know that he was wasting his time keeping track of me.

Where was the ex-cop anyway? I had to keep reminding myself that it was still entirely possible that Ray Sargent had shot Dewey and Lamar Boone. Had loaded the money into his car, then saw me coming and decided to wait. To see if I were worth killing.

Something about the man had me believing his story, however. The handcuffs lapel pin? His gravelly voice? His heart condition?

Perhaps my irrational faith in his honesty was my own worst enemy. Sometimes you just had to hate people who tell the truth. I rolled down my window and enjoyed the night air. It smelled like freshly cut grass. If someone was following me, I wished they'd stop me and tell me where I was going.

My new suit was neatly folded over a chair. I sat on the motel bed, watching television. I didn't have cable at home. Here, they had it all, including the Playboy Channel. Corinne was in the bathroom, mixing new drinks from the bucket of ice I'd dumped into the lavatory sink. She came back into the room with a plastic (guaranteed sanitary by the management) glass in each hand, Johnnie Walker Black on ice.

Corinne wore only panties. She giggled when she saw what was on television. When she giggled, she also jiggled. Corinne was loosening up. Earlier, she'd asked who'd done my tattoo. Now she was once again looking at my chest.

"People call you Rooster?" She handed me the drinks and crawled onto the bed. Sitting next to me, Corinne took her drink back.

"Cock-a-doodle-doo," was all I said.

"I was thinking of getting one," she said. "A tattoo."

Corinne slipped a piece of ice into her mouth and

bent over my belly. She licked me. My stomach muscles instantly tightened. Corinne, I decided, was insulted that I was watching television. I drained my Scotch and let it burn down my throat, spreading to my chest. Then I poured the ice over her head.

"Shit," she said, jumping up, jiggling, spilling her drink on the bed. "What'd you do that for?"

"I want to talk."

She sat pouting, rubbing her hair. Then she grinned as if nothing had happened.

"Okay," Corinne said. "Some guys want to talk and some guys want me to talk. Some want to talk before. And some want to talk after. What do I care?"

"Sounds like you've been around?"

"A lot."

"You know Dewey Boone?"

She didn't say anything.

"Or maybe I should ask if you *knew* him?"

"Maybe I heard of him." Corinne was being too cute. She hadn't been around at all.

"Do you like to eat turds, Corinne?"

She stared at me without reply.

"You know, human feces? I could ask you to eat my shit if I wanted to. And you know what would happen to you when you got back if you refused, don't you? I mean, you've been around, Corinne. You know what four hundred dollars buy. Four hundred dollars buy you, Corinne. You're bought and paid for."

"Yeah, well, I don't eat shit." She crossed her arms over her naked breasts. Her nipples had drawn into hard red knots.

"But you could learn. If you *had* to."

"So, Dewey Boone's a nobody who turned up dead. That's all I know. He your brother or something?"

I stared at her, my brown eyes against hers.

"Really!" she insisted. "Word is he was some guy that pissed off some other guy and now he's dead."

"You read that in the papers?"

"I don't have to read the paper to know what's going on."

"Way I understand it, he got killed for his money."

"Maybe," Corinne said, shrugging. "I don't know about that."

I believed her. "You ever roll over for him, Corinne? You ever give it away to Dewey Boone?"

She shook her head no.

"Who's Rosalinda?"

Corinne laughed. She uncrossed her arms. "What, are you writing a book or something like that? Cause if you are, I don't want to be in it."

I waited.

"She's somebody's daughter or granddaughter. The old man named the place after her. At least, that's what they tell. She sure as hell don't hang out at the house."

"The old man?"

"Yeah." She paused. "You know!" It was as if by saying his name she might evoke his presence.

"Morelli? Leon Morelli?"

"Yeah, Leon. The old man."

Leon was the reputed don of the Kansas City mob. Both sides of the state line. I'd never doubted that his reputation was based on fact. His nephew, Andrew, worked for Sam Geolas. Everybody who worked for Sam Geolas was somebody's nephew, now that I thought about it.

"Rosalinda's his granddaughter, huh?" I was busy thinking. Putting two and two together and coming up with four hundred thousand.

"Word is she doesn't have anything to do with him or his friends. It's a big joke that the old man named the place after her. They had some blowup years ago."

I knew it! Rosalinda was a woman. A smart woman. A beautiful woman.

If Dewey Boone had known her, I could find her. I remained stone-certain that he'd been speaking of a woman when he'd spoken of Rosalinda. I was up from the bed, pacing, telling myself that I should just lie down and go to sleep. That it was better than spending the night at my place or curled up in the seat of my Datsun.

"Hey," Corinne said cheerfully, "you ready for another drink?"

Chapter 15

The phone rang. Without thinking I rolled over and picked it up.

"What?"

"Rooster, tell your girlfriend to take a bath."

It was a voice I immediately recognized. The television was on. Corinne was asleep, curled into a ball next to me.

"Wrong number." I hung up and unplugged the cord jacked into the base of the telephone. It was 4:22 A.M. I woke Corinne by shaking her.

"Go into the bathroom," I told her. "Keep the door closed and run some water in the tub. Hurry!"

"Huh?"

"Run the shower and don't open the door."

She didn't understand.

"Corinne," I snapped. "A man is coming through that door in the next two minutes. If you see him or if he sees you, there's a good chance somebody will end up dead."

"Huh?" She rubbed her brown eyes.

"Coke deal," I lied.

"All right already," she relented. Corinne uncoiled herself from the covers and stamped off in her bare feet. She slammed the bathroom door behind her. I put on my pants and waited. Didn't this guy ever sleep? I didn't believe Ray Sargent would shoot anybody, but you had to say these kinds of things to women from time to time to get their attention.

Ray Sargent wasn't a tall man, but he dressed like one. He looked lean and well-cut in his dress shirt, slacks, and jacket. You had to admire the way he wore the .32 in his right hand as he came into the room. I locked the door behind him, feeling extremely under-dressed. Ray's handcuffs lapel pin caught the light of the dresser lamp and winked at me.

"Have a seat," he said in his gravelly voice. He smiled politely, not quite disturbing his silver mus-tache. "Nice tattoo," he added, referring to my shirt-lessness. I sat on the edge of the bed and studied the gloss on his shoes.

"We getting any closer?" he asked.

"Closer to what?"

"Retirement."

"I'm beginning to think the mob has the money."

"It's a possibility." Ray Sargent leaned against the dresser, playing with his gun. As always, he held the automatic .32 very casually; yet, he managed to keep it pointing in my general direction at all times.

"Oleta Pryor took a powder," Ray told me. "What do you think about that?"

"What do *you* think about it? You're the security consultant."

"I wondered briefly. I really did, Rooster. I won-dered if she was in on it. But hell, we know better than that. The FBI doesn't, though. They followed her to some beach in Florida. Seems her boss . . . uh, Mr. Foster, is also headed in that direction. You know, what's a little robbery when you've already made plans?"

I shrugged.

"The FBI is wrong sometimes," Ray continued, "and sometimes they're right. Take you, for example."

I looked up.

"They talked those Okies into letting you loose and then almost had to buy some dirt-road county a new patrol car."

Maybe, I thought. *Maybe* he's telling the truth.

"They're on to you, Rooster. They just don't have any evidence. They want the money, son, and if it all comes up empty for them, they'll send you away on that stolen-car charge. They don't give a damn about it, but they'll do it anyway. Out of spite."

"You come by this time of night to tell me to be careful?"

"Just thought you might have learned something by now."

"I learned that you got my apartment watched."

"Not at all," the ex-cop protested. "Just me. I drive by once in a while. I know your hours, Rooster. I know when you're there."

"So you're in this alone, is that it?"

"All by my lonesome, Rooster. I tell you no lie."

I coughed. The water ran in the shower. I hoped Corinne didn't open the door.

"Well?" he asked after a pause.

"Well, you know as much as I do."

"But we're not giving up, are we?"

"No, we aren't," I snapped. I rubbed a hand through my bed-tousled hair.

"I talked to a Miss Krebs recently," he said, watching my reaction.

"I hope you didn't follow *her* home."

"Can't handle the hot ones. Bad heart."

He waited for me to say something. I waited for him.

"I told her we thought you might've pulled the job on her bank."

I looked up quickly and couldn't help but grin.

"So, I admit she was dumb about it," he said. "Not a bad shot, though. Sometimes you guys make mistakes like that, Rooster. Sometimes you tell the woman."

"Sometimes we don't."

"But it's not a bad idea, is it? Checking out the women?" Ray Sargent nodded toward the bathroom door, behind which Corinne kept the water running as

I'd instructed her to. "They don't like being left out of things," he added. "You take off and leave a woman behind and she's just dying to talk to somebody about it."

"Wynona is a woman of action, not of words." I wondered briefly if she'd told Ray Sargent about my secret room.

"But you know what I'm saying?"

"Dewey Boone?"

"Or Leon Morelli. There's all kinds of women in a man's life."

"So I hear, so I hear. Sisters and mothers, grandmas." I smirked. Why didn't this old guy do his own legwork? It ate at me that he might already know about Rosalinda. Then again, he might not.

"Hey," he said, "it's your money."

"Once I find it."

"For as long as you can keep it." Ray Sargent wasn't smiling when he said it. He pulled away from the dresser, walked across the room toward the door.

"Nice suit," he said, pointing his gun at my clothes across the back of the chair. "By the way, Rooster, the FBI's not tapping your phone. But someone else *is* recording your calls." This time he grinned broadly.

"Up yours," I said as he opened the door and walked out. The door didn't quite close. A moment passed. Ray pushed the door open again from the outside. He stuck his head inside the room. Ray Sargent spoke loudly and clearly.

"I'd keep my eyes open for a couple of strongarms in a Trans Am if I were you. They aren't nice fellas, Rooster."

"Thanks," was the only thing I could think to say. Thanks for nothing. This time the door closed. The man sure did like to talk.

Time chased me. In the person of Ray Sargent. The FBI. Two mobster hoods in a gold Trans Am. Outstanding warrants for my arrest in Oklahoma. And

Dewey Boone's ghost. They were all ghosts stalking my soul. Ghosts with teeth, ghosts with guns.

I put on my suit, draping the red tie loosely around my neck. I left twenty bucks on the bed and told Corinne to take a cab. She was snoring but would probably figure it out. I drove in a rush, forcing myself to watch the speed limit. At a 7-Eleven just off I-70 north of town, I borrowed a copy of the Greater Kansas City Telephone Directory. The white pages. Thumbing through the phone book, I felt like a hound chasing leaves blown by the feckless wind.

There were more than a dozen Morelli listings. But only one *R.* Morelli.

The address was 3703 Locust, a few blocks north of the University of Missouri. I walked outside to the phone booth and dialed her number. I kept getting my quarter back. Rosalinda wasn't home. At five in the morning, Rosalinda wasn't home.

Rosalinda's area was a peninsula of older homes kept up in a torn neighborhood. There were a number of stately apartment buildings from the twenties. The old folks, however, had held their ground. They gave in by occasionally renting a room of their large houses to students. I had every reason to believe that Leon Morelli's granddaughter was a student. I'd hoped she'd be older.

Since she wasn't home, I concluded she was either at a boyfriend's place or that she was out of town. Unless she was enrolled in a summer course, school was out. I had my fingers crossed that Rosalinda was academically ambitious.

I parked in a reserved-parking lot outside the library. Inside, I had to kill fifteen minutes before the library opened at seven A.M. Instead of waiting, I hiked quickly across campus to the student union, where I'd met Dewey Boone. At a row of pay telephones I found what I wanted: a university directory.

Strangely, there was no Rosalinda Morelli. There was no R. Morelli. There was no Morelli.

I drove up Locust, toward 3703, and I almost ran into it. The Kansas City Art Institute.

Bizarre, sharp-cornered sculptures decorated the grounds. I drove onto the campus of the small school. Avoiding the building that looked like a dorm, I parked illegally in front of a low brick structure with the sign ADMINISTRATION. Inside a glass door, I asked an elderly woman behind a desk if she could help me locate Rosalinda Morelli.

She flipped through a stapled stack of photocopied schedules.

"Studio," she said. "Studio all summer."

Across the street from the Art Institute were two large stucco houses serving as studios for senior students. I followed my directions to Studio A. I walked inside the open door.

Chapter 16

I had goose bumps. My palms were sweaty, my throat dry. I felt as if I were about to discover gold. Pieces of broken furniture were all over the place. A car bumper. Pottery shards. Paper and string. Rope. Bags of plaster. I stepped around a sleeping dog and walked upstairs. Three doors opened off a narrow hall. I thought of the short story they made me read in junior high, called "The Lady or the Tiger?"

What if behind all three doors there was no lady?

I thought of *Let's Make a Deal*.

The first two doors were locked, making my choice much easier. I knocked on the third door, which was painted blue. In white letters someone had painted *Genius at Work: Steal Silently Away*. Behind the blue door, a radio played softly.

Opening the unlocked door, I looked inside. The room was large and sparse of furniture. A deep sink was on one wall, and the wall opposite the door was windows. Another wall was lined with shelves. A huge table, covered with supplies, took up a good portion of the open space. In the middle of the rest of the room sat a couch with the stuffing exposed on the arms.

On the couch, a woman slept.

Rosalinda was curled on her side; her butt, pointing right at me, invited me in. She wore gray sweatshorts and I could see the lace border of her panties. I came inside.

Pinned to the wall above the sink were large works of paper, the paper saturated in pastel blue. I stepped closer to the wall for a better look. Painted on the blue surfaces were intricate figures, the backgrounds sketched in with charcoal. The watercolor figures were the bodies of women, and all their faces were blank. Projects in progress, I surmised. Rosalinda was quite talented.

"You like?" a woman's voice asked.

I turned around to see Rosalinda sitting up on the couch, her knees drawn to her chest, her toes hugging the outer edge of the cushion. She wiggled her toes. She wore a T-shirt without sleeves. The rest of her hid behind her drawn-up legs.

I'd pictured Rosalinda dark and beautiful, with Spanish eyes and long, black hair. Full red lips. I'd guessed wrong. Rosalinda's colors were blond and pink. And a very light blue, her eyes. Her eyes were blue like diamonds are blue. Rosalinda's hair was cut short, too short. But her diamond eyes, her eyes were magic! Large and wide and curious. Sparkling. I wondered briefly if she could ever tell a lie.

"Well?"

"Perhaps," I said, trying not to stare at her openly. "But the question is whether you like."

I didn't want to scare her with my intensity. My heart raced, but I forced myself to remain outwardly as calm as possible.

She scratched her short hair and opened her knees. Rosalinda's gray shorts gapped, exposing the crotch of her panties, the covered secret of her sex. She looked at me like a cat, watching. Her eyes never blinked.

"I don't like," she finally said, as much to herself as to the stranger standing in the middle of her studio. "I haven't been able to do anything all year. Not a god-damn thing."

Her paintings were, in fact, quite striking. Quite good. They touched something in me and, in turn, caused me to want to touch them, to touch the surfaces of her art with all my fingers. But there would be time to tell her that. Or so I ardently hoped.

"Let's get something to eat," I suggested out of the blue.

She looked at me, cocking her head slightly.

"Do I know you?"

"Alton," I said, surprising myself with the truth. "I write," I hastily added.

"Wrongs?"

"Words," I lied. I thought about telling her I was free-lancing for an art magazine or something like that. Rosalinda closed her knees and rested her chin in the cradle they formed. Her hands wrapped around her calves and she hugged herself, rocking, staring at me with her diamond-blue eyes.

"You're not a writer," she proclaimed.

I raised my eyebrows.

"Because you're too interested in me. I saw the way you were looking at my work."

I smiled. She smiled. Smiling was a start.

"Okay," she said.

"Okay what?"

"Okay, let's get something to eat."

With that she jumped to her feet and took me by the hand. Without a pause she led me from the studio. At the door of the house she left me waiting while she dashed back upstairs to find her shoes. It might have been the money that made me nervous, but I felt as if I'd finally met the girl in the yellow dress.

Later, in my truck, Rosalinda tied my red necktie around her neck. I drove to the Corner Restaurant in Westport. She wore the tie into the café. Seated in their back room, Rosalinda ordered the vegetarian quiche. I had ham and eggs, greasy hash browns.

"Rose," I said. "I want to ask you about Dewey Boone."

She sat on her side of the booth on crossed legs. Rosalinda looked up at me with such sudden anger that I expected her to leap to her feet and walk out on me. An intense hatred filled her eyes.

"Linda," she said very cooly. "Linda, not Rose." She returned her attention to her food.

"Okay. Linda it is."

"You're him, aren't you?" Rosalinda did not look up from her quiche.

"Who?"

"Frank something or the other. The man who got Dewey killed. I told him not to take the money. But they killed him anyway. He was always talking. Dewey told everybody about it and they killed him."

Rosalinda was crying.

I struggled to swallow a bite of my eggs.

"And now you!" she sputtered. "You want the money. Jesus Christ, this is ugly. Real ugly."

If my heart could have talked, it would have screamed. I sat silent. I scraped my fork around the surface of my plate.

"I'm sorry," I forced myself to say. "I didn't know." It came out as a hoarse whisper.

When she looked up at me, Rosalinda's eyes were red and wet, but the crystalline blue shone through. Even crying, Rosalinda's eyes could have pinned Wild Bill Hickok to a tree and held him there overnight. He'd have been helpless, unable to reach for his gun, his horse, his hat.

"Just tell me you're not working for them. 'Cause

if you're working for them, I'm leaving the fuckin'
country. I swear I am."

I reached across the table and touched her hand.
Rosalinda couldn't stop crying. She let me take her
home.

Standing at the windows, which ran from the floor
to within a foot of the ten-foot ceiling of Rosalinda's
apartment on Locust, I looked out across the street. A
small modern-brick building on the corner turned out
to be the regional headquarters of the Boy Scouts of
America. An American flag fluttered in the breeze. An
empty cardboard box, pushed by the wind, tumbled
across the Boy Scouts' parking lot.

I turned from the window. At a time like this a
man could tolerate only so much of a good deed daily.

Rosalinda's bed was on the floor of her third-floor
walk-up, half of it covered by open magazines. Books
were stacked along one side of the bed. An overflow-
ing ashtray was within reach of the pillow at the head
of the bed.

Boxes stuffed with all kinds of things made up the
rest of the room's furnishings. Under one of the boxes
was an easy chair. A table with a yellow Formica top
and heavy chrome legs filled the apartment's small
kitchen.

Just off the kitchen was the bathroom, its door
open. Tiptoeing back into the front room/bedroom, I
tripped over a gray and white cat. Soundlessly the cat
ran into the kitchen.

Rosalinda was taking a bath. She hadn't asked me
to stay, but she hadn't said that I should leave. I studied a variety of paintings, drawings, and mixed-media
mounted on the walls of the apartment. Not hers, I
concluded, but the works of friends. I knew how that
went. I wanted to remember to ask Rosalinda if she
ever wore a yellow dress.

I listened to the muddled sounds of water splash-
ing in the bathroom. My blood ran hot, then cold, as I
thought about the murder of Dewey Boone and his

uncle. I wasn't responsible for his death, I decided. The man who pulled the trigger was.

In a larger sense I had been in charge. I was responsible somehow. I couldn't erase the sick feeling by swearing upon my Boy Scout's honor to be trustworthy, loyal, brave, and obedient for the rest of my life.

As each minute went by, it became more important for me to get to the money. I couldn't let the bastards who'd killed Dewey Boone have it. Soon I was back at the tall windows, wondering where all the Boy Scouts were at ten in the morning on a given Thursday. She called my name. I walked into the kitchen.

"Yes?"

"Get me something out of the fridge to drink, would you?"

The refrigerator was crammed full of cartons and sacks and unsealed packages. A bottle of white grape juice. Two loose cans of different brands of beer. A half-empty bottle of cheap, white wine. And a glass of what had probably once been orange juice.

"Beer?" I asked.

"Fine."

I closed the door, holding the available cans of beer. "Want me to roll it through the door?"

"No." She laughed. The water sloshed. "Bring it on in. I want to talk."

I expected to find her standing just out of the tub, wrapped in a towel. But Rosalinda sat in the tub of steaming water, her elbows on its porcelain ridge. Rosalinda's hair was wet, as was much of her skin. I handed her a beer, trying not to stare down at her.

The large, footed tub was deep enough to stack five or six bodies in. Rosalinda's knees were drawn up, poking through the water like islands of flesh and bone. Her breasts, seeming to float on the surface of the soapy water, were larger than I'd realized. Buoyant. Her nipples, tightened into pointy knots, looked as if they'd be hot to touch.

Rosalinda was not shy about her body. She opened and drank from her can of beer. Her cat scrammed, leaving us alone in the small, damp room. I was looking for a place to sit, a place to look besides at her.

"Thanks," she said casually. As if she'd been handed the salt at the family supper table. She glanced up at me. I blushed. Her lips were full and beautifully pink. Rosalinda was a painting of a young man's fantasy. The most perfect, glistening colors I'd ever seen, though my favorite color was dollar-bill green.

I sat on the only available seat, the toilet, and opened the other beer. I gazed out the open door into the kitchen, embarrassed. Rosalinda seemed fully at ease. As if nudity were natural and something you didn't have to hide.

I grinned at my shoes. "I don't feel like a stranger," I blurted out. "You ever spend time in jail?"

Rosalinda laughed, a delicious, deep-throated music. Her laugh.

"You think I have the money, don't you?"

Her question surprised me. "No. I don't, but I think you hold the key to finding it."

"I know who's got the money," she insisted. "And so do you. It's probably been laundered already through one of the casinos in Vegas and is on its way to Colombia in exchange for a couple million worth of uncut coke."

"*They* didn't get the money. Dewey didn't take it with him. Or if he did, he hid it somewhere along the way."

"How do you know?"

"He left a message."

"And what was that?"

"Your name."

Rosalinda breathed in deeply. I looked up quickly. She smiled at me as if to apologize.

"Don't worry, Alton, I'm through crying."

"You were in love?"

"Something like that. Dewey was a real sweet guy. And yeah, I guess I loved him. But what I loved about him was that he was so innocent. You know what

I mean? Kind of like a puppy or a cat. But you could never have told him that."

I nodded, then looked away. I could see just the top half of Rosalinda's white breasts from where I sat. Her skin sparkled. I wanted to taste it and I knew she could sense that.

"He came around sometimes. He liked to stay up late and I always stay up late. He didn't know who my grandfather was. I told him I was from St. Louis and that I wasn't related to the Morelli family here in town. He believed that for the longest time."

"But they found him. Were they watching you?"

"Oh, no, not really. Dewey had his connections. He kind of found them. He thought he was going to be this big-time coke dealer, some fancy dude that all the girls would just die to spend some time with. So, he'd practice. You know, he went around strip joints and tried to sell coke to the pimps and stuff like that."

"Playacting?"

"Training is what he called it." Rosalinda let her knees slip under the surface of the water, stretching out her legs, leaning her head back. "At the last minute he'd tell them the shipment didn't come through but that he would let them know."

"And?"

"And I talked him out of doing it."

Rosalinda sank into the water until just her face was above the surface. "But not in time. You go around Kansas City talking about dealing coke and sooner or later they're going to make it a point to talk to you."

"Your grandfather's people?"

"If you can call them people." She closed her eyes, sinking deeper. Soon, Rosalinda's entire face was submerged. Then she rose slowly from the water, until her pliant breasts bobbed to the surface again. Her empty beer can floated on the water in front of her.

"And that was that? He told them he was robbing a bank?"

"Probably," Rosalinda said. "It was his reason for not dealing snow. They told him they'd heard he was dealing coke and he probably said, 'Not me, man. I'm robbing banks.' "

Rosalinda smiled at the thought of Dewey Boone's having said that.

"And you told him not to do that, too?"

"No." She sat further up and looked right at me. Her breasts, lifted fully out of the water, didn't droop an inch. "I told him not to take the money. I didn't tell him not to rob the bank."

"That doesn't make sense," I managed to say.

"Maybe." Rosalinda stood up in the tub. I waited until she'd dried her legs and had wrapped the towel around her waist before trying to talk again. Rosalinda slipped a clean T-shirt over her damp head. Her face popped out grinning. She let the towel fall to her feet. The hem of her purple shirt covered, just barely, what had to be covered to keep me from grabbing her young body by both cheeks and burying my face in Rosalinda's blond nest.

"What about four?" I said. She used a fresh towel to dry her short, blond hair. "Dewey said you told him his lucky number was four."

"Yes." And that was all she said.

I followed her through the kitchen and into the front room. She sat on the edge of her bed. Rosalinda squeezed body lotion from a plastic bottle and began to slowly massage it into her legs, rubbing each from ankle to thigh. Then she sat back on the bed with her legs crossed and lifted her T-shirt over her head.

I watched in awe as Rosalinda rubbed lotion over her entire torso, paying tender attention to the flesh of her breasts.

"This is when I go to bed," she said, as if to explain.

"You're driving me crazy."

"I know."

Chapter 17

I wondered if Rosalinda's urgent saying hello to me among the linens of her bed was simultaneously her way of saying good-bye to Dewey Boone. It didn't matter, though; I was in heaven and it felt good too.

That's what I liked about women. No two were exactly alike, and neither were any two entirely different. Rosalinda, however, was an incredible exception. She was a little bit of every woman I'd ever known, and it all added up to something one hundred percent different. I couldn't get enough of touching her or being touched by her.

The only drawback I could think of as I kissed the dimple in her chin for the hundredth time was that her mattress wasn't made out of four hundred thousand dollars' worth of crisp bank notes. I must have been getting dizzy because the longer I was with her the less important the money seemed.

Still, the money was there, somewhere. It had become a part of me and nothing Rosalinda and I did made me forget that.

Sex with other women had been something like driving around in bumper cars at an amusement park. A lot of fun, don't get me wrong; but with Rosalinda, I was in control and wholly out of control at the same time. To put it bluntly, we fit. Perfectly. Over and over again. Our bumper cars crashed into each other and stuck. I explored every inch of her with every inch of me.

It was dark before we rested. Rosalinda lighted a cigarette; she glowed in the dark. I often enjoyed the smell of someone else's burning tobacco. I lay back and listened to my raging pulse telling me that this time it was different. She'd been making love to me. Dewey Boone was dead and buried.

Rosalinda's cat walked across my face, and I didn't move. It seemed at the time like a very normal thing for a cat to do. The stars, I knew for the first time in my life, were where they belonged. The man the cat walked on wanted nothing more than never to have to leave the bed. Though he knew he would leave to find the money.

Rosalinda started laughing.

Quietly at first and to herself, she laughed. It sounded like a stifled cough. Then Rosalinda couldn't stop. She laughed and laughed and bubbled with more laughter. I touched her with my hand and felt the spasms of her laughter. I wanted to be inside her while she was laughing, but I didn't move. Eventually she stopped, only to erupt into a burst of out-of-control giggles.

It seemed right that she should do that, and I didn't have to ask.

"I know it's stupid," Rosalinda said, "but I can't help it." She giggled again and had to stop talking. "I guess I'm just happy. My body's happy."

Rosalinda broke out laughing again, doubling over on the bed, trapping my hand in the fold of her body.

Soon her laughter was a muffled cough again. She'd come full circle to the beginning. Rosalinda sat back up. I tried to look at her, but she turned her face away as I did and screamed, "I'm a chicken, I'm a chicken!" And I was laughing too. We were stoned. We were each other's hallucinogenic drug. The cat fell off the bed.

"I kept picturing myself laying all those eggs," Rosalinda explained. "It was like a cartoon. Since you're a rooster and all, I'm a chicken." We both got a good laugh out of that. It felt great, falling in love. The Boy Scouts across the street could hang their good deeds on the flagpole if they wanted to. I already felt helpful, courteous, kind, and clean all over.

"You know," I told her. "You know that I knew it would be like this? Even in jail I knew it would be like this."

Rosalinda looked at me as if we'd known each other forever.

"Yeah," I went on. "Being with you. I knew it all along. I've been waiting since my mother turned the radio on and left me on a blanket in the middle of the floor to fall asleep. I must have been three, maybe four, when I started waiting for you. Those old songs told me all about you."

I was in the bathtub and Rosalinda was in the kitchen, going through the fridge for something to eat.

"You know what I want?" I called from the bathroom.

"What's that?"

"I want to look at your body and your face forever! And I want the guys in the Trans Am." All I heard in reply was the refrigerator door slam shut.

Rosalinda wore a white cotton robe, tied with a crimson belt at the waist. She stepped into the bathroom and stared at me with her clear blue eyes, her hands on her hips.

"I don't believe you," she lamented. Then she marched out, muttering to herself. And then she marched right back in. "Just tell me one thing, Rooster Benjamin Franklin. Just one thing!"

"What's that?"

"If ignorance is bliss, how come you aren't any happier with the way things are?"

It wasn't a question; it was a rhetorical demand. Rosalinda trooped out again, flipping off the light. I slumped lower into the tub to think about things. I heard the refrigerator door open and close. In a moment the light in the bathroom came back on. Rosalinda stood with a fat bunch of celery held over her head. I ducked just in time.

The celery bounced off the wall behind the tub and plopped into the water.

"Men!" she shouted in exasperation. Rosalinda

threw up her hands and stormed once more out of the room, turning off the light as she went. I sat in the darkness, inhaling the perfumed bubble bath. It was sort of fun, I thought, this being in love. I hoped she didn't find a jar of peanut butter to go with the celery.

I shook the water from the celery and snapped off a small stalk. I stuck it in my mouth and chomped.

Later we lay back on the bed, Rosalinda in her robe, I in my pants. She was playing a record she wanted me to listen to, by some group called X. I asked if she could get the oldies station on her stereo, which played from inside a cardboard box.

"This *is* old-time rock 'n' roll," she explained. "You have to listen to the lyrics."

Before the song was over, we were making love again. We moved together gently at first, but before long our lovemaking turned into a passionate and tormented slamming of ourselves together as we each became a part of the other.

Our bodies exhausted, slickened with sweat, Rosalinda and I couldn't stop. Wouldn't stop. It was as if we were one machine grinding on and on and on . . . Until she called my name one more time.

"You," Rosalinda said, when we were finally through, "are something to crow about."

We lay silent, watching the night lights come through the window and move shadows that looked like waves across the ceiling. Cars driving by. We were quiet for the longest time and I must have dozed off. I heard the refrigerator come on.

"You can't go to sleep?" I finally asked.

"My body doesn't want to."

I found Rosalinda's hand and brought it to my lips, kissing her fingertips. "Alton," she said, "there's something different about you."

"Us," I said, correcting her. "What's different about me is you."

"There's something special here, isn't there? Something besides Dewey's death. You know what I mean?" She turned in the bed to face me. "You feel it, don't you? It's like I'm vibrating very quietly all over."

"Like we've known each other all our lives?" I offered.

"Yes, that's it. But I don't know you, do I? I don't know anything about you."

I told her everything. I told her about a kid in Oklahoma quitting school so he could hang around with the older guys in town. The hoods. I told her about a kid who got caught holding eighteen cartons of cigarettes behind a closed grocery store at two in the morning.

"What did you do?"

"I ran. At least, I started to. The cop leaned out his car window and told me he'd use his gun if I didn't stop."

"And?"

"And I believed him."

"What about your friend? The one inside the store."

"They got him, too. He joined the navy."

"And you went to prison?"

"It wasn't my first offense," I said. "There'd been other things. Small things. Stupid things. Eventually, though, they get fed up with you and away you go."

"What things?"

"Getting drunk and driving around the countryside in the back of a pickup, tossing a lasso around every mailbox we came to, pulling them up by the roots of their posts. By the time the county stopped us, we had thirty-seven mailboxes in the bed of that truck."

"They put you in jail for that?"

"It all adds up. Besides, I was a dropout. The judge probably figured I could use a little educating."

"Is that where you got your tattoo?"

"Uh-huh. The guy was an artist. He was in his eighties. It was a privilege if he agreed to do one for you. Had the steadiest hands of any old man I'd ever met. Trouble was, he did what he wanted. He said I reminded him of a rooster and that's what I got. Worked off and on for months finishing the colors."

"Did you pay him?"

"No. He did it because he wanted to. He did it because I was young. It was his idea of immortality. The old joker said that when he was dead, his tattoos would still be out there getting in trouble."

"And here you are," Rosalinda said spritely. "Getting in trouble."

"Rose," I said, but she stopped me.

"Linda," she insisted. "My grandfather calls me Rose."

"Do you hate him?"

"I think so," Rosalinda confessed. "When my father was shot down in Union Station, shot in public to bleed to death on the floor, something inside me snapped. Something broke that can't be fixed. I couldn't stand to look at my grandfather. It was all his fault. It was the way he'd brought up my father, to take over the family, that killed him."

She paused, then spoke very softly. "I wanted to change my name. But then I thought I'd keep it and make something out of it. Morelli doesn't have to mean what it means to people in Kansas City."

She talked about her painting. About her mother, who'd taken the money Rosalinda's grandfather, Leon Morelli, had offered her. Her mother lived in Boston now, married to an English professor. She talked about her watercolors on pastel blue.

"I never do the faces. I don't know why. The faces just aren't there. I can't explain it, Alton. Either the faces are there or they aren't. And they aren't. It isn't something you can force your hand to do."

"I know." And I did know. "It's like the face of my father. I used to try and picture it when I was a kid. I'd never met the man. I'd never seen him and he'd never seen me. There's just this face that isn't there."

Rosalinda sighed deeply. "Yes, that's it exactly." She moved against me. Rosalinda's skin was cool on that warm and humid June night. A breeze came into the room through the open windows.

I told Rosalinda about my secret room.

"I thought you were a thief," she said, her voice a small sound. Rosalinda slipped her arm around me, her head against my chest. I could feel the air of her breath on my skin. She kissed me lightly, very lightly.

Then Rosalinda was asleep, and quietly I told her more of my story, not wanting her to wake up.

Chapter 18

Rosalinda was still asleep when I dressed and left in the morning. I thought to leave a note saying that I'd be back. I didn't. She'd know.

It had rained and the sky remained overcast. Bright patches of green grass looked lively between the dull reds and grays of the buildings as I drove across town toward Thompson Street. I turned right on Rainbow Boulevard from Forty-third, north one block to turn left on Forty-second Street.

Winchell's Donuts was on the corner, my apartment six blocks away. Driving by, I saw a familiar figure crossing the corner parking lot, walking from a slate-blue '84 Camaro. I turned the wheel of my Datsun pickup sharply and drove into the lot. There was something I wanted to say to the dapper gentleman walking in that door.

Pulling into a slot in front of the window, I stayed put until he'd been waited on. While I waited, a black-and-white Kansas City, Kansas, patrol car pulled up. Two young, uniformed officers got out. I followed them in. He wouldn't be able to hold a gun on me this time.

"Nobody deserves nothing," Ray Sargent told me when I asked him why he thought he deserved the money from the robbery. The two police officers sat across the room, ignoring us. "I know about the money is all. And I get my chance." Ray looked tired.

"I'm your chance," I said, scoffing.

"No, *I'm* my chance. You have to take your own chances."

"With the FBI, for instance?"

"Maybe them, too."

"No, not the FBI," I said harshly. "That was your smoke screen. There is no FBI. *You* called on Carolyn in Wichita. *You* got me released from jail in Oklahoma. I don't know how you did it, but you set up my escape. Probably flashed your antique badge, said I was wanted for murdering a busload of children in Missouri. That the only way to convict me was if I led you to the murder weapon."

My voice shook with anger. It had taken me too long to catch on. Even now I was playing a long shot, but Ray Sargent's response would give me the answers.

He looked up from his donut and coffee. As soon as our eyes made contact, I knew I was right.

"Keep your voice down," he urged. "I did it for your own good."

"My good or *your* good?"

"I didn't want you to go to sleep on the job. I wanted you up on your toes and running. I wanted you to work, Rooster. I wanted you to sweat. You see, we aren't the only ones after that money. You slack off too long and they'll beat us to it."

"But you got your money on me, right? You really believe I know where it is, don't you? You think I'm just hanging around till the coast is clear and then I'm going to drive somewhere and pick it up."

I worked hard to keep my voice down. I was seething.

"Those boys in the Trans Am are real, Rooster. I'm not the only one watching you. You've got to understand that. They aren't going to be polite when they corner you, you understand?"

"Well, they're as wrong as you are. Dewey lost the money and he's the only one who knows where."

Ray Sargent searched my angry eyes for a glimmer, for a sign that I might not be telling the truth.

"So what are we doing this for?"

"We're doing *this*," I said mockingly, "because *this* is my life. *This* is what I do, officer. You're the one that's hanging around doing nothing."

He ate a bite of his donut, chewing slowly, watching over my shoulder. There was a dust of donut sugar on his silver mustache. He sipped from a styrofoam cup of coffee. It looked as if it had gone cold.

"They beat up the girl," he told me. "The prostitute. She told them everything."

"How do you know?"

"Tea and sympathy, Rooster. It goes a long way in this world. I got there a little late, that's true. But the girl needed a friend for an hour or two. They now know everything I know. They know you found Rosalinda."

"They won't touch her. She's blood."

"True." Ray Sargent smiled slyly. "But tell me what makes her the good guy in all this."

I strangled the urge to throw Ray Sargent's coffee in his face. Instead, I sat there and shook with anger. The police officers got up and left. I couldn't have cared less. I was capable of killing the old man with my bare teeth.

Ray Sargent wasn't smart enough to let up.

"She could have set him up," he said. "Dewey could have trusted the wrong woman. And Rooster, she could be setting you up, too."

I jumped to my feet. My hands clutched the back of the plastic chair. I wanted to explode into violence against Ray Sargent's person. I wanted to punch him in the face. I wanted to bounce him out the glass window and run over his legs in my truck.

"I'm sorry it bothers you to consider this," he said

slowly, carefully. "But you better start using your head, son. The boys in the Trans Am were at your apartment early this morning. My guess is they tore up the place. My guess is, Rooster, if you'd have been there, the only place I'd be following you to today is the graveyard."

I didn't say a word.

"Think it through, cowboy," he pressed. "If somebody's got the money and it isn't you . . . who is it? Who did Dewey give it to?"

"There's only one thing I want from you," I hissed, leaning across the small table.

"How can I help?"

"I need the name of an honest cop. A detective on the Missouri side. Somebody who'll bust these boys in the Trans Am if I don't kill them first."

"Morelli's in tight, Rooster. The prosecutors are afraid of him. What you need is a federal agent."

"No. All I need is a cop. I ain't after Morelli. I'm after the guys who pulled the trigger on Dewey and his uncle. And I'm going to get them. One way or the other, I'm going to get them. You'd just better pray, old man, that it wasn't you."

"Warren Felker." Ray Sargent took another bite of his donut. I walked out.

I drove into my parking space behind the apartment building on Thompson Street. It was home, but something told me I wouldn't be living there much longer. As I walked by the Dumpster, something caught my eye: a surgical glove, used, the fingers inverted. It had been tossed toward the Dumpster in a hurry. Or it had fallen from a sack of trash.

Students at the University of Kansas Medical Center lived in the building, I reminded myself. Yet, the glove worried me. I unlocked the security door and dashed upstairs to number 18. Ray Sargent was right; the door to my apartment was unlocked.

I pushed it open cautiously to discover that my apartment was, as Ray Sargent had predicted, a total mess. The furniture had been turned upside down. A lamp lay broken in the middle of the floor. My coat closet had been emptied. From the front room I could see into the kitchen. My trash had been strewn all over the place. The refrigerator door was open.

Then it hit me. My secret room!

I rushed past the bedroom and found the door to my other room kicked off its hinges. As I stood in the broken doorway, I realized the stereo was on. They'd turned the radio up to cover their noise.

My studio was destroyed. Racks of costly oils had been spilled. A tube of red paint had been stepped on, bleeding into the carpet at my feet. My workbench was toppled. Sketches were torn into pieces. My few canvasses had been cut with a sharp knife or a razor.

It wasn't the mess or the destruction that bothered me. It was, simply put, the invasion of my privacy. The assholes had gone too far, they'd stamped on my secret life. I felt as if my deepest being had been violated. I felt as if someone had dug up my mother from the grave and had tossed the body parts around the room. It wasn't right that those creatures knew this secret about me.

Then I discovered they'd gone much further than that.

A body was in my bedroom. I recognized the crazy Hawaiian shirt from the doorway—the pattern of large white sailboats on a background of two-tone-blue waves. The shirt had always been Paul's favorite.

Paul Valley sat on the floor, his back against the bed. Paul's eyes were closed, his mouth open. A puddle of blood bathed his tongue. His head lolled awkwardly backward on the edge of the bed. There was nothing I could do to breathe life into his body.

Paul's hands were tied, behind his back, and his ankles too. His shoes were off and his pants pockets had been turned wrongside out. I didn't have to look any closer to know that the other side of his head had been shattered by a .32-caliber bullet fired at close range.

Why?

I pictured them interrogating him. I could hear Paul Valley telling them to go have sex with cattle, that he didn't know anything about the Heartland robbery, about the four hundred thousand they were after. Then I could hear him telling them they'd made a mistake.

And asking them not to kill him. Then pleading. *They'd killed him to get to me.*

My head rang. I gagged. Tears burned my eyes.

I had to get out of there. I had to think about other things than how I was going to tell Carolyn about this.

I reached down and picked up a package of matches. A spot of blood obliterated the name of the motel—a place in Indianapolis. Paul had been on his way home. He'd come by to find me not there. He'd picked the lock, which he was pretty good at, and made himself at home. He'd wanted to talk to me.

I also picked up Paul's ring of keys.

They weren't going to get away with this. The ringing in my ears turned into a savagely painful headache. I made myself turn away from my best friend and walk out of the room. I locked the door to my apartment and walked to my truck as if in a trance.

I drove without turning on the radio. I found myself parked outside the fence of the airport runways, watching the jets take off and land, a pint of Johnnie Walker to my lips. Drinking it in straight, large swallows didn't burn enough. It couldn't burn enough.

There wasn't enough fire in that bottle to erase the image of Paul Valley's death-face. Not enough fire to burn away the color of Paul's blood from my inner vision. The sound of the gunshot I hadn't heard echoed in my brains. The blast tore a large chunk of me away. My guts lay all over the cab of my truck.

My headache worsened.

Dammit, Paul, why didn't you stay on the road one more lousy day?

A jet was taking off, coming right at me. The people inside had their belts fastened, heading somewhere different. Some were going somewhere new, others were returning home. Jets flew in circles. I rolled the windows of my Datsun down, letting the huge noise wash over me in a great shaking wave. But it didn't wash the pain away any more than the liquor had.

I pictured Carolyn in her quiet bookstore in Wichita, telling a gray-haired grandma which of the books were good to read. I pictured Carolyn missing him more than she'd ever missed Paul before. But not as much as I missed him.

For the moment that money seemed worthless. Except that it was vital that I get it instead of the dirty bastards who'd killed my best friend. I had to have it, for Paul, even if I ended up burning it in the fireplace. It was *our* goal, Paul's and mine.

Driving back from the airport, I felt a new, horrible pain. I thought of how fragile a life my daughter must be. I thought of the soft skin stretched over the inside of her wrists. I wanted to find her and protect her from all this. But other things had to be done first. Things just now occurring to me.

I wanted to know their names, the boys in the macho-mobile.

Chapter 19

Things happened fast. By the time I put the Datsun in my parking place at the Thompson Street apartments, I had a plan. I walked around two buildings and the pool and climbed into Paul Valley's battered '68 Ford pickup. He'd left it parked on the street in front of my apartment.

The body of Paul's truck was slitted with rust, but he had the thing in good running order. The aluminum camper shell would come in handy as a place to store my gear. I drove to the 7-Eleven on Thirty-ninth Street and bought a newspaper. I read the classifieds until I found the ad I was looking for:

REMINGTON—12 ga. pump, $185.

I called the number and told the man who answered the phone that his shotgun was sold. He gave me directions to his house, which turned out to be near the Venture's department store on Roe.

Kansas had no waiting period for the purchase of shotguns, and no required registration. I paid cash.

The man who sold it to me told me the slipcover went with the gun. I told him thanks, but without much sincerity. The things only cost two bucks. He told me I needed a new truck, and I told him that if he didn't shut up I'd come back later to steal his. He thought I was kidding.

The radio in Paul's truck worked, for which I was thankful. The straight AM job was okay by me. The oldies station WHB was 71 on the AM dial. Somebody was singing that he still could see blue velvet through his tears as I pulled into Venture's parking lot. The store boasted a large hardware department.

I purchased forty feet of clothesline rope, two pulleys, and brackets. I bought a sack of nails and a new hammer. Only the fact that I was down to less than a thousand in cash kept me from picking up a medium-size chainsaw.

In Sporting Goods I found a water-shed sleeping bag. I bought a folded hunting knife. And I asked for a box of .00 magnum 12-gauge shells.

"Only got number twos," the guy at the counter said.

I told him that would have to do.

"Wrong time of year to be huntin' goose," he said, ringing up my purchases.

"There's a bear been running through my trash," I said. "That fucker's getting too close, you know what I mean? Makes me nervous, what with the kids sleeping outdoors and all."

The Remington held five shells. One direct hit with extra-powder 2-shot would blow the door off a Trans Am at fifty yards. My shopping cart was nearly full and I was making my way to the door when something caught my eye. At the radio counter I bought a Polaroid SX-70 and four packs of film.

I turned the corner with my cart and ran smack-dab into a sunglasses display. I selected a pair with red-and-white-striped frames for Rosalinda. Before I got out of the place, I was left with about six hundred dollars in my wallet. If I wasn't more careful, I'd wind up cashing in one of Avery's savings accounts or having to steal a couple cars before this thing was over.

On the way back to the Missouri side of Kansas City, I put on the red and white sunglasses. I stopped for booze, my only appetite since discovering Paul's body in my bedroom. On a whim I added a half gallon of milk and a box of Cap'n Crunch to my booty. Again, for Rosalinda.

Back in the truck, I broke the seal on my Johnnie Walker. Just drunk enough to feel rushed, otherwise I would have sat in the parking lot and finished off the bottle in my effort to drown Paul's ghost.

I entered Rosalinda's apartment building and climbed the stairs. Wearing her sunglasses, I knocked on the door, and knocked some more. Rosalinda wasn't home.

I drove Paul's rattling truck through the Art Institute campus. I could have made it at a place like this, I thought. I could have been a damn good seventh-grade art teacher somewhere in the hills of Tennessee if I'd have thought of doing it in time. Funny thing, if I hadn't gone to prison, I would never have known that I possessed the desire to paint. Or the talent. Prison gave you time to discover things about yourself.

As I turned onto the block of the two stucco houses that served as studios, my heart froze in my chest. The gold Trans Am was pulling away from the curb.

I got a good look at the two junior mobsters as

they drove by me from the opposite direction, from in front of Rosalinda's building. The passenger was small-built with a blond crewcut. He looked like a Nazi inside his leather jacket.

The driver was larger and older. He had jet-black hair combed straight back and wore black-lensed sunglasses. He wore what looked like a French-cut silk shirt, also black. I couldn't tell whether the shirt had no buttons or whether he simply wore it open to his navel by choice. There was a glint of what looked like gold chains around his neck. I figured he would run about two hundred and fifty pounds.

I'd seen them both before, of course. Parked in front of my apartment the night I'd gotten back from Wichita, my first night back in town. This time I looked them over more closely. This time they looked more menacing.

Rosalinda's sunglasses must have thrown them off. Or maybe they hadn't noticed Paul's truck parked in front of my apartment.

The killer sat in the passenger's seat. I knew it by looking. Don't ask me how, but I knew he carried a .32 inside his leather jacket. What I also knew, and didn't want to know, was that the boys in the Trans Am had been visiting Rosalinda. They were acquaintances. And it was suddenly very possible that she had set up Dewey Boone.

Loving a woman worth her salt is flying an airplane with a landing gear that won't go down. Sooner or later, you crash. But the plane doesn't explode; it doesn't burn. It leaves you in bloody pieces with a broken back. You long for the jungle animals to come along to chew away something vital. Loving a woman worth her salt isn't over until you're dead.

Chapter 20

I couldn't run from it, so I ran at the heart of it. As I topped the stairway, it occurred to me that they might have been here to hurt her. That the mobsters might have been working Rosalinda to get to me against her will.

Yet, when I opened the door, Rosalinda looked fine. She smiled at me as if she'd been eating sunshine.

I slapped her as hard as I could. Her sunglasses flew from my face. Rosalinda crumpled, fell back into the studio without making a sound. My hand stung. She dropped to her knees and slumped over to her side. Rosalinda's hand covered her face.

I heard Rosalinda release a small sob. Her hand trembled. Still, had she risen up, I would have hit her again.

I strode into the studio and closed the door behind me, locking it. I picked up the candy-striped glasses and put them on. Turning my back on Rosalinda, I stared at the faceless figures on the wall. I wanted an explanation, but I wasn't going to ask.

"I'm sorry," she said to my back. Rosalinda's voice was surprisingly strong and sharp. She cleared her throat. She took a deep breath. "Whatever they did, I'm sorry."

Sunglasses or no sunglasses, I couldn't make myself turn around to look at her.

Paul had wet his pants. In fear or in death, he'd soaked his pants with his own hot urine. Somebody was going to pay for that. For the blood that ran down the side of his face and discolored the front of his favorite Hawaiian shirt.

"I want to know their names," I said between

clinched teeth. My stomach hurt. I needed another drink.

"They were looking for you," Rosalinda said. "Not for me." I could feel her blue eyes searching my back for understanding.

"Their names!"

"I told them I didn't know where you were or when . . ." Rosalinda's voice cracked.

"Their goddamn names, Rose! Now!"

"I love you," she yelled, and Rosalinda began to weep. "You were safe with me," she blurted out. "Don't you understand that? They won't touch you while you're with me. They wouldn't dare."

I nearly turned around to look at her. Instead, I stepped away, across the room until her worktable was between me and Rosalinda.

What it felt like to hit a woman, a woman you cared about, was what it felt like running over a kitten in your truck. I felt untrustworthy and disloyal. I felt wholly disobedient, glum, wasteful, cowardly, unclean, and irreverent. I was a pisspoor Boy Scout.

And still, I would have hit her again. I would have picked her up by the shoulders and slammed her trembling body against the wall. Paul meant that much to me. I would have hit her and hit her and hit her . . . until she told me their names.

Rosalinda had been in her studio for quite a while. She'd been working on a drawing. Lying flat on the table, the drawing was a shaded sketch of a tall man between two tall trees. Rosalinda had tried to do the face. She'd finished the eyes—my eyes looking up at me from the piece of paper. It was worse than a mirror.

I looked down then at Rosalinda looking up at me. Her eyes were red and her face was streaked with tears, but she didn't appear frightened. She only looked hurt. I threw the red-and-white-striped sunglasses across the studio. They clattered against the wall and fell like a duck taken out by the blast of a .12-gauge.

Rosalinda could not hold my stare. Perhaps there was too much hate in my eyes. She averted her gaze.

"Norman Purdy," she said, her voice a hoarse whisper. "Norman Purdy and Marco Morelli."

I wanted to throw something big. I wanted to pick up the couch or the table and hurl it out the window. The blond punk was a relative—her cousin or worse. I walked to the lavatory basin against the wall and ran cold water into my cupped palms. I rinsed my face. The headache hung in there.

Rosalinda was saying something. As I turned around slowly to look at her, she remained on her side on the floor. Rosalinda talked to the wall.

"They're going to kill you," she said. "They're going to kill you. They're going to kill you."

"Your brother?" I asked.

Rosalinda nodded her head, not glancing away from the wall. Outside the clouds spread, uncovering the sun. Bright daylight filled the studio. He didn't make sense, God and His weather.

"I'm sorry," I said.

Rosalinda looked up, her reddened blue eyes wide with wonder. She was reacting to the amount of pity in my voice when I'd said I was sorry. It was clear to her that I wasn't apologizing only for having slapped her, but for what was going to happen.

"Do you own a dress?"

She nodded. Her face was flushed. I looked away. What was all this light doing in the room? I wanted the sunglasses back.

"We're going to the police." The tenor of my voice did not allow her to consider my statement as anything other than pure fact. There was no choice for her to make. I walked to the door and unlocked it.

"Now," I said, opening the door of her studio. "Right now."

Rosalinda stood up as if in a trance. I longed to hold her, but I wouldn't let myself. There was work to be done. Paul was dead. I had to be strong enough to see this through.

I followed her down the hall, down the stairs. I touched her shoulder once we were on the sidewalk and Rosalinda stopped. I opened the passenger's door of Paul's pickup and she climbed in.

The murdering bastard was Rosalinda's brother, and she was going to help me kill him. Or she was going to help him kill me. Whether she liked it or not, Rosalinda was involved.

I drove to her apartment on Locust and waited in the truck for her to change into a dress, panty hose, and a decent pair of shoes. I waited for her to come back down and climb into Paul's Ford pickup, beside me. There was no question that she would do otherwise.

I took another hit of Johnnie Walker. I didn't feel any better, but it kept me from feeling a whole lot worse. I didn't want to do this to Rosalinda, but Paul was worth the all of it. Not that I'd ever forgive myself, not that I'd ever forget. Sometimes the only thing you were given was a chance to get even. Norman Purdy and Marco Morelli were going to pay.

Chapter 21

Major crime cases in the greater Kansas City area were often handled by the so-called Metro Squad. This was because of the state line that separated jurisdictions. And because of the numerous smaller communities, making up the metropolitan area, that didn't have adequate investigative branches of their own. The criminals ignored state lines and city limits.

I called Lieutenant Warren Felker from the lobby of the municipal building. I was relieved to hear a voice say "Metro Squad" when the phone was an-

swered. Felker was in. I told him a girl named Morelli
wanted to sign a complaint.

"She can do that at the desk," he said gruffly.

"Maybe you didn't hear me, Lieutenant. I said
Morelli. As in Leon Morelli. There's a couple of things
we want to talk over with you."

"You her lawyer?"

"Boyfriend."

"I don't make deals, boyfriend. If you're after
some kind of deal, call the district attorney's office."

"No deals."

"Come on up then," Lieutenant Felker said after
a pause. "Third floor, end of the hall on your right." He
hung up the phone without giving me the opportunity
to speak.

Lieutenant Warren Felker had his own office, a
small metal desk, no windows, four wooden chairs, and
sixteen file cabinets. A picture of his wife and three
little lieutenants sat atop the metal desk.

Rosalinda sat down primly in a chair facing the
desk. The bottom black button of her blue dress was
open, and her legs looked delicious behind the gap.
Lieutenant Felker was getting us coffee. He came into
the room holding two styrofoam cups.

"I'm afraid it's not very fresh." He handed one
cup to Rosalinda, the other to me. "Both had sugar,
right?"

"Thank you," Rosalinda said, staring at the picture on his desk.

Lieutenant Felker had swept-back graying-blond
hair and a full mustache that drooped over the corners
of his mouth. In his late forties, he wore a dark-brown
pinstripe suit with a similar cut to the suit jacket I had
on. Only his wasn't as wrinkled as mine. He wore a
striped blue shirt with a white collar and a navy-blue
tie dotted with tiny red specks. The pindots were so
small the tie looked purple upon first glance.

I liked him better seeing how poorly he dressed. I
had serious doubts, however, about the woman in the
picture on his desk. There was no wedding band on

Lieutenant Felker's left hand. The wife was an ex. The kids were people he visited every other weekend or less.

Lieutenant Felker sat down behind his desk, rubbing his mustache with one hand. "Rose Linda Morelli, is that right?"

"Linda," Rosalinda said.

"And what is it that I can do for you?"

I sipped my coffee and stayed out of it. Rosalinda knew what to say. We'd gone over it.

"I want to sign a complaint. Two men have been harassing me at my home and at my studio, and I want them to stop."

"Studio?" Lieutenant Felker asked, leaning back in his chair.

"I'm an art student at the institute."

Lieutenant Felker thought about it for a moment, then held out his hands. "Why me?"

"Your name was given to us by an anonymous friend," I said. "He said you were honest. He said you were the one who'd care enough to look into it."

"Harassment? I'm on the Metro Squad. We work major cases. Now, I would be happy to assign someone to drive by your apartment now and again, Miss Morelli."

"There's more," I interjected.

Lieutenant Felker arched his eyebrows. "And who were you again?"

"Her boyfriend. Albert Barnsdale."

"I see. You ever steal a car, Mr. Barnsdale?"

I looked away from him.

"You look just like somebody I watched go in and out of a front for stolen cars. What was your first name again?"

I didn't say anything.

"Did you tell me your name was Rooster? Or was it something like Alvin?"

Rosalinda looked at me. I still didn't answer. The police detective had my sheet. They'd staked out the Good Buy Tire Store. They'd seen me and they'd looked me up. They'd asked around. If they had something on me, I wouldn't be allowed to leave. My guess was that it was all a coincidence. Lieutenant Felker couldn't connect me with the Heartland Savings & Loan robbery.

"Let's not bullshit around," I suggested. "You know who Leon Morelli is. And you know who Rosalinda is. And you damn well know who Norman Purdy and Marco Morelli are."

"So tell me something I don't know, Rooster. How about you do that?"

"Norman Purdy and Marco Morelli have been harassing Rosalinda. She wants it to stop."

Rosalinda was silent now.

"And what else does she want?"

"There was a murder in Hot Springs, Arkansas. A man named Dewey Boone, a student at the University of Missouri here, and his uncle were shot to death," I told him.

"I've got some paper on that."

"Norman Purdy and Marco Morelli are the men who did that."

This time the lieutenant was quiet for a second. "She swear to that?" he asked, nodding at Rosalinda.

Rosalinda shook her head no.

"Consider it a tip, Lieutenant. You won't get Rosalinda on the stand. Her grandfather hires mean lawyers."

"So what good is all this?"

"You have to catch them," I lied. "And when you do, it will be worthwhile to look into the Hot Springs murders. That's what good is all this." I was going to catch them for him.

"We don't investigate out-of-state murders, Rooster."

"There's something else," Rosalinda said, interrupting.

Both the lieutenant and I stared at her. She spoke calmly, looking him in the eye.

"They robbed the Heartland Savings and Loan

courier," she said, shocking both of us. "My brother and Norman told me that."

I didn't know if she was saying it for my or for Dewey Boone's benefit. But I could have kissed the woman right then and there. I felt like asking her to dance.

"And you know where the money is?"

"No," she said flatly. "The money's gone. It financed something big. That's all I know."

I wondered if she was telling the truth. If Norman Purdy and Marco Morelli had scored the money, they wouldn't be after me and they wouldn't have murdered Paul, I decided. She was making it up.

"And you won't testify to any of this, Miss Morelli?"

"She won't," I answered for her.

Lieutenant Felker rubbed his mustache again. "I should throw you both out."

The room was hot. A tickle of sweat ran down my back. I could smell the Johnnie Walker seeping out of my pores.

"What about this murder, Miss Morelli? Do you agree with your boyfriend that your brother and a guy named Purdy had something to do with it?" It bothered me that Lieutenant Felker had already known that Rosalinda and Marco were sister and brother. I must have been the only guy in town who had to beat that information out of a woman I loved.

"I don't know anything about it," she said.

"How about this Dewey Boone? You know anything about him?"

She shook her head no.

"I should throw you out," Lieutenant Felker repeated. "Both of you."

Instead, he handed each of us a copy of his card. In turn I gave him the personalized plate of the Trans Am, Macho III. I started to give him a physical description of Norman Purdy and Marco Morelli, but the lieutenant told me he knew who they were. Lieutenant

Felker's home number was on the cards he handed to us.

"Now, let's go down the hall and fill out the paperwork on that harassment complaint," he offered.

The idea was that, by signing a complaint against her brother and the mob's wheelman Purdy, Rosalinda would be in the clear when the real trouble hit the streets. When I put my plan into action. When Norman Purdy and Marco Morelli turned up dead outside her apartment building or inside her studio, or when I turned up dead, Rosalinda would be on record as having nothing to do with it. Of having done her best to keep her family's business from tainting her.

The cops and the crime reporters in town already knew that Rosalinda had struck out on her own. They were already aware she had severed ties with her grandfather and all that he represented.

What I hadn't considered was pinning the Heartland job on her brother and Norman Purdy, pinning it on the mob. The cops would jump at that. They'd believe it even if they could never prove it, even if they never came up with enough evidence to prosecute. Rosalinda had come up with that stroke of genius on her own.

"You got a lot of balls to come waltzing in here, Rooster, with that girl on your arm," Lieutenant Felker told me as Rosalinda signed the formal complaint. "We could look into things."

It was my turn not to say a word.

"Your record isn't exactly what I'd call clean," he added.

"Sam Geolas buys stolen cars. You know it and I know it," I said quickly. "It's not up to me to do anything about that."

"No, it isn't," Lieutenant Felker said angrily. "But I would stay the hell away from him from here on out."

It wasn't the cars they were after. I knew that much. If they'd wanted Geolas on fencing stolen cars, they could have busted him already. There were bigger things going on. Geolas was in tight with the mob.

Lieutenant Felker wasn't in charge of that; the Organized Crime Commission had control of Sam Geolas's
fate.

   Still, I knew good advice when I heard it. I'd stay
away from Sam and his Good Buy Tire Store. In fact, in
a few days I'd stay away from Kansas City altogether.
I'd talk Rosalinda into leaving with me.

   As we drove back down Broadway, the golden
dome of a church spire caught the sunlight. My headache was back. Rosalinda held her hands folded into
tight fists. Any minute, I thought, she was going to
smash me in the face with both hands. She stunned
me, however, in another way.

   Rosalinda slid over on the seat and kissed me on
the cheek as I stopped for a red light.

   I needed help with Paul's body. Rosalinda was the
only person I could trust.

   We sat side by side in a booth at Twin City Tavern
on Forty-third Street and the state line, less than a
dozen blocks from my apartment. Twin City was on
the Missouri side. Unlike Kansas public taverns, Twin
City served drinks. Twin City also sold a lot of carryout
beer on Sundays when the bars in Kansas were closed
by law.

   Kansas was a backward state when it came to
making money off of society's bad habits. To have fun
in Kansas you lived near the state border.

   Rosalinda and I kept our backs to the door, watching the room. Two guys in T-shirts were shooting pool.
Another couple were watching television at the far
end of the bar. A pleasantly plump blond in shorts and
a sweatshirt approached our booth.

   "Walker Black and a Bud back?" Marci asked.

   I nodded.

   "A glass of white wine. . . . No, make that a gin
and tonic." Rosalinda looked at me and said, "I never
know what to drink."

   It was dark in the booth. The only lights were

behind the bar, over the grill, the jukebox, and the light above the pool table.

Marci brought us our drinks. Rosalinda rested her head on my shoulder and sipped her gin and tonic through a narrow plastic straw. I took my ounce and a half of twelve-year-old Johnnie Walker left-handed, in two swallows. My right hand was in my lap, holding Rosalinda's splayed fingers against my leg.

"I meant what I said when I told you I loved you," Rosalinda said softly. "I don't understand it, but I do. It's there. Something inside."

"Like a tumor?" I suggested.

"Like a blossoming tree. Like a tree reaching to touch the sky."

I drank from my bottle of Bud. Marci knew I didn't use a glass and hadn't brought one for me. I liked the feel of the wet bottle and the damp label in my hand.

"Will you tell me about your past?"

"I already have," I said. "When you were asleep."

"Tell me now."

"The present right now is smothering me; I can't think about the past. How old are you?"

"It doesn't matter," Rosalinda insisted.

"What does matter?"

"That I'm telling you the truth. I haven't been with a man in over a year. I just got fed up with the whole thing, you know? But you made me want to do it again, Alton. There's something about you. Your past."

"You and Dewey were, uh, just friends?"

"Something like that." Rosalinda squeezed my leg. Marci came back with another Bud for me and a fresh gin and tonic for Rosalinda. I would only get more Johnnie Walker when I asked for it. I put my feet up in the empty seat across from us. Rosalinda's hand was high on my leg now. I could feel my secret self stretching, like Rosalinda's metaphoric tree, to touch her nearest finger.

Then I thought of Carolyn. And of Paul.

"Tell me about your brother," I said.

Rosalinda lifted her hand from under the table. She picked the slice of lime from her finished drink and sucked on it, her pink lips swelling over the green rind. She squinted her eyes with the sourness of the fruit.

"We're blond," she said. "That's one thing. Seems the patriarchy in the Morelli line had a taste for blond women. My grandmother was blond. My mother was blond. And it finally showed up in Mark and me."

"You might not get along with the rest of the family in Italy."

"Oh, we'd be the hit of the party. Grandfather always thought we were special. We got exorbitant gifts on our birthdays and at Christmas."

I peeled a corner of the Budweiser label from my beer.

"I'd been to Europe three times by the time I was sixteen," she said.

"What went wrong?"

"I found out who Grandfather was, what he did for a living, when my father was killed. Grandfather kept telling me someone had to be in charge and that he was better than most."

"You believe that?"

"It doesn't matter. I hate him. If he'd been a plumber or a used-car salesman, my father would still be alive. Then I'd have a *family*."

"So would Dewey Boone still be alive," I said, and probably shouldn't have. And so would Paul Valley. Of course, they'd both still be alive if I'd pulled the Heartland robbery alone.

"Yes," she said quietly.

"Your brother," I kept on. "What if I kill him?"

Rosalinda shrugged to mask her reply.

"He deserves it," I said.

"You can kill Norman Purdy, if you want to. You can get even that way." Rosalinda meant that I wasn't allowed to kill her brother. But her brother, I took it, was allowed to kill me.

"Do you have a sister?" Rosalinda asked.

"I have a daughter."

"I know."

"I thought you were asleep when I told you about that."

Rosalinda held her hand over the table, fingers outstretched, and flipped it casually from side to side. "Off and on," she said.

I finished my second beer and in moments Marci was back at our booth. Rosalinda accepted her third gin and tonic. Three I decided was the right number. She'd have to be a little drunk to help me with Paul's body.

"Why don't you kill the old man?" Rosalinda suggested once Marci had returned to watch television with the couple at the end of the bar. "My grandfather's responsible for all this. He killed Dewey Boone."

"Maybe I will," I said, thinking I had no real grudge against the old man. "But each man is responsible for his own sins."

"Speaking of which, why don't you show me where you live?"

It was after three P.M. It was Friday. Twin City would be filling up with people in an hour or so, people getting off work.

"Finish your drink," I suggested. "We'll be leaving soon."

"Your place? Can we make love where you live this time?"

"There's someone at my place."

"Wife or girlfriend?"

"A dead man. My best friend." We finished our drinks in silence.

Like father like son, I discovered. Marco was in management training with his father's company. Currently he was in charge of the whorehouse on Garfield. I decided he might be able to help me with a little problem, the body of a friend.

Chapter 22

My place. Rosalinda was nervous. I'd told her
about Paul Valley on the way over. It had felt good to
talk about it, but as we climbed the carpeted stairs to
my apartment, there was nothing to say. I'd backed
Paul's truck up to the rear security door so that it
would appear as if someone were moving in or out of
one of the apartments.

I unlocked my door and pushed it open. Rosalinda
stepped inside ahead of me. I reached behind her and
turned on the lights.

"You keep it nice," she said, forgetting for a moment the gravity of the situation. The apartment did
look as if it had been the scene of a demolition derby.

I left her standing in the middle of the room and
ran downstairs. I brought out the water-shed sleeping
bag from the back of Paul's camper. Upstairs I found
Rosalinda standing in the broken doorway of my secret room. She'd turned on the light.

"Your work is very strong." She studied the sliced
canvasses from where she stood. "You paint with
strength and verve."

"Painted. Past tense."

"Really," she insisted. "This stuff is alive. Better
than Matisse. Stronger. Like Gauguin brought in-
doors."

"More like Alton Franklin in prison," I allowed.
"Which is where we'll both end up if you don't give
me a hand in the other room."

Paul's appearance hadn't improved any. He sat in
his bloodstained Hawaiian shirt where I'd found him.

Rosalinda watched from the door as I unzipped
the sleeping bag and worked Paul's body inside of it.

"I'm so sorry," she sputtered.

140

"Your grandfather didn't put the bullet in his head," I reminded her. Her brother had. I didn't mention that.

"They thought he was you?"

"Maybe at first. But no; they killed him because they thought he had the money. Or that he knew something about the money. They killed him because they're rotten lousy stinking dirty bastard assholes who like their guns, and they figured nobody would give enough of a fuck to do anything about it. They did it to scare me."

I huffed and puffed around the words as I zipped up the bag. I couldn't have done it without her standing there. I couldn't imagine what I would tell Carolyn. But I knew what I would do next. Paul was going to play a special part in Norman Purdy and Marco Morelli's night of justice.

"Are you?" Rosalinda asked. I stripped the bed. I rolled up the sheets and the blanket into a large cloth ball.

"Am I what?"

"Scared?"

"Not enough. Not enough to let them get away with this."

Rosalinda lifted his legs as I'd instructed her to. The top three black buttons of her cobalt-blue dress had come undone somewhere along the line. As she bent over, I could see the smooth tops of her breasts. Sex and death, I thought. Sex and death.

It was true what everyone had said. Nothing made me want to have sex more than picking up the body of a dead friend. It wasn't horniness. It was survival, desperation.

Paul's body was hardening, but the joints weren't locked.

We had to stop twice on our way downstairs. Rosalinda helped me place the body in the back of the camper without saying a word. I ran back upstairs for the blanket and sheets and for a change of clothes.

I also picked up my leather purse of lock-pick

tools. The expensive ones. And a new pair of surgical gloves. I finished off the bottle of Johnnie Walker from the glove compartment. The days were getting longer. It wouldn't be dark for another two hours.

I soaked inside Rosalinda's deep bathtub. I was looking forward to not having to wear my suit jacket, my dress pants. A pair of my favorite well-worn jeans were waiting in the other room, a cotton Kansas City Royals T-shirt.

I slipped down in the tub until my face was underwater. I was baptizing myself, washing Paul's death from my body. I wondered if Ray Sargent was waiting outside, whether he'd seen us load the body at my apartment building. Probably.

I dried off, rubbing my hair with a towel. I wrapped the towel around my waist and stepped out of the bathroom. Rosalinda was doing something in the kitchen. She'd taken off her blue dress and her black shoes and was holding a champagne glass in her hand.

Her lips tasted like wine. Rosalinda climbed onto a kitchen chair to kiss me, to look me in the eyes, to throw her arms around my neck. I hoped Ray Sargent was enjoying this.

"Women should be as tall as men," Rosalinda said, kissing me again, leaning her hard-nippled breasts against the damp skin of my chest. Rosalinda struggled out of her white panty hose.

"You should date jockeys," I replied. Rosalinda poured her glass of white wine down my bare back, causing me to do a little dance. As I squirmed inside her arms, I pressed against the entire length of her body. Rosalinda opened her legs and clung to my neck.

Then her legs lifted around my waist, the bathtowel falling to the floor. She'd managed to bring our sex together.

"The window's open," I said.

"Screw the Boy Scouts," she whispered.

Rosalinda pressed her pelvis against mine, and my hands reached around to hold her buttocks up, to keep her from slipping to the floor. We kissed deeply as I carried her in that position into the other room. We fell, locked in coital embrace, onto her unmade bed.

The lights were out in this room. The curtains closed.

I lay on my back, thinking how much Paul would have enjoyed this. Rosalinda lowered herself on top of me and I forgot all about Paul as I reentered her, as she rocked back and forth, bending to kiss my lips.

Then she stopped moving. She sat back on her haunches, still holding me inside her. Her blue eyes stared at me, darkened in color.

"Rooster, you're not here. You're not with me."

"The part of me you need is here. My best friend is dead. He should be getting laid by someone like you."

"Shut up and don't feel guilty for good things." Rosalinda slipped away from me. She kissed my belly. She took me inside her mouth. I tensed at first, then forced myself to relax as she worked her hands under me.

I called her name as I released a small army of hot, white ants into her mouth. Rosalinda turned her back to me and curled into a ball with her hands between her legs. She cried.

I reached to touch her.

"I don't want to come," she said clearly. "I just wanted to make you happy. I wanted to make you forget your friend. To forget my brother and my grandfather and to forget about the money."

"I can't," I admitted in the darkness. My real release would come, I knew, when I closed my finger on the trigger of a shotgun pointed in the right direction. We fell asleep alone, inside ourselves.

When I woke up, the room was darker than before. It was raining again. It seemed as if it would rain every morning and every night until I left town. Rosalinda held my hand, sleeping heavily. We had become sleepers joining hands. I'd heard of that happening, but it had never happened to me before.

As I dressed, mad at myself for having forgotten to bring along a more comfortable pair of shoes, I wondered if all the ants were dead by now. If one or two were still struggling inside her body, struggling against mortality.

I opened the curtains and cracked the window, feeling the breeze from the evening rain. What I was about to do wouldn't be easy. I was going to give up Paul's body, give it back to them.

Across the street they'd taken down the American flag from the Boy Scout parking lot. A lighted sign on the side of the building reminded us all to do a good deed daily, but there were no merit badges for getting your best friend killed. I flipped my middle finger at the rain.

I walked along the 800 block of Garfield Street, Kansas City, Kansas. I wore the translucent, skintight, skin-thin rubber gloves made for surgeons and their nurses. I'd put on Paul's jacket, retrieved from inside the camper of his truck. It was blue and shiny, with the word KANSAS in large red letters across the back.

I stopped behind the gold Trans Am parked in front of Rosalinda's plywood sign. Men went into the house and left with clocklike regularity. I wondered briefly if Corinne had left her job there after having been bruised by the macho mobsters Norman Purdy and Marco Morelli.

A car's trunk was tough to pick, but patience usually paid off. The trunk of the Trans Am surprised me by popping open at the very instant I was certain my pick was breaking in half. I brought the lid down and left it gapping by an inch. I ran back to Paul's pickup, parked around the corner.

The streets were wet but the rain had stopped. You didn't get summer in Kansas without a week or two of evening thunderstorms. I backed Paul's truck up behind the Trans Am, parking it on the wrong side of the street. The tailgate of the pickup was a foot from the open trunk of the gold Trans Am.

I removed Lieutenant Felker's card from my pocket. On the back I'd scrawled a message: *Look in the trunk.* Holding the card in my teeth, I left Paul's truck running out of gear with the emergency brake on, then ran around to unload the sleeping bag containing Paul's body into the waiting trunk of the macho-mobile.

Paul was heavy. I had to pull his knees up and push him over sideways to get the trunk closed. Paul's wallet was inside the bag with him. Skipping around to the front of the Trans Am, I placed Lieutenant Felker's card under the windshield wiper on the driver's side.

Back inside the cab of Paul's truck, I glanced at the loaded .12-gauge pump on the floorboard. "Be right back," I told the lighted ROSALINDA sign in the rearview mirror as I pulled quietly away. I kept my gloves on just in case. I didn't know how much time I had. Maybe the management of Rosalinda's played poker in the back room until dawn. Maybe not.

There was a Quick Trip convenience store on Tenth Street. I pulled my truck up to the drive-by phone and I dialed 911. An operator came on the line to inform me that 911 was for emergencies only. I asked for the police.

"Kansas City, Kansas, dispatch," a male voice said. "Police Department."

I took a deep breath, then shouted excitedly, "Officer down! Garfield Street! Officer down!"

"Your location, please."

"Gold Trans Am, Kansas license personalized Michael-Alpha-Charlie-Hoboken-Oscar, roman numeral three. Rear windshield blown out by officer fire."

"Hoboken?"

"H, dammit. It's *H.* I have an officer down!"

I hung up the phone. When you called 911, the line remained open until the call was traced. I

wouldn't be there when the phone rang, when the
police showed up to take fingerprints.

The police responded to one thing like no other,
and that was one of their own dead or dying. As soon as
the dispatcher was on the police band, they'd show up
in droves, racing up and down Garfield Street, looking
for a gold Trans Am. I had my own racing to do.

This time I stopped Paul's truck in the middle of
the street with the headlights on. Carrying the shotgun, I skipped around the truck and camper to stand
directly behind the gold Trans Am. I held the shotgun
tightly against my shoulder, careful not to rest my
cheek on the stock.

The gun jerked violently backward with the blast,
the roar of the .12-gauge waking up the night. Dogs
began barking. The rear windshield of the Trans Am
evaporated. Someone shouted from the porch of
Rosalinda's. I lifted the gun one more time and
worked the pump, ejecting the empty shell while the
mechanism automatically replaced it with another. I
blasted a hole through Rosalinda's plywood sign.

I picked up my empties after pumping the shotgun again.

Throwing the gun into the cab, I jumped in behind it, slipping the running pickup into gear before
getting the door closed. I popped the clutch and
squealed the rear tires on the wet pavement. I was a
block away in no time. I turned the corner and parked,
shutting off the lights. I also kept my foot off the brake
pedal to keep the red brake lights from giving me
away.

I watched as the junior mobsters ran across the
front yard of the whorehouse, both carrying guns in
their right hands. Norman Purdy stopped a few feet
from the car, afraid perhaps that someone was waiting
for him. Marco Morelli's face turned from side to side
as he surveyed the street in both directions. He
pointed in my direction.

Then Marco shouted something and they both
rushed the Trans Am. Someone had seen the camper

from the house, had told them it was a guy in a pickup who had pulled up and shot out their rear windshield. I wondered if it had been Bernice in her fancy underwear and fishnet hose.

I couldn't drive away before the cops showed up because the mobsters would follow me out of the strike zone. But I couldn't just sit there either.

Shoving it into first gear, I popped the clutch again. I hoped Paul's transmission held up. I stepped on it—the accelerator, then the brake. I slid on the wet pavement around the corner of the short end of the block. I thought for a moment the camper would turn over. It didn't.

I heard sirens.

I was at the end of the block as the Trans Am screamed around the corner, chasing me. I turned again. And again. And I was back on Garfield, speeding by Rosalinda's red hand with a black hole in it. I was also speeding directly toward two black-and-white patrol cars racing right at me, one behind the other, sirens on, red lights flashing. A third was another half-block behind the first two.

I pulled over to the curb with a quick jerk of the wheel but kept moving. I pulled back into the street as the first two wailing police cars raced by, missing the rear end of a parked Seville by inches. I turned the corner and was off the block before the third police car got there.

A huge whirling noise permeated the night as a bright spotlight shone from the sky—the police helicopter.

If I hung around, the cops were going to stop me. But I wanted to see it. I circled the block again, more slowly. As I approached the intersection of Garfield, two more patrol cars raced by, from the opposite direction of the first three. They had the Trans Am trapped. My plan had worked.

But what would they do with me? A guy wearing surgical gloves, with a warm shotgun on the floorboard and two spent shells rolling around under the seat,

wasn't going to be listened to. Should they find the
bloodstained blanket and sheets, I'd be in jail without
bail.

I pulled up to the corner and rolled the passenger's window down to get a better look along Garfield.
I had the lights off, but I kept the engine running. The
Trans Am was sideways in the street, blocked in and
illuminated by the spotlight of the hovering helicopter. The uniformed officers were out of their vehicles.
A hell of a lot of shouting was going on—then gunfire.

I saw a figure jump from the driver's side of the
Trans Am. Red spits of gunfire lit up the dark corners
of the night. The hunched over figure of Norman
Purdy stood directly up and then collapsed backward
against the car. The helicopter spotlight illuminated
the body. Police officers rushed Norman Purdy's collapsed form. Another distant siren approached.

Two uniformed officers rushed across the lawn of
Rosalinda's, crossing in front of the sign. They leapt,
one after the other, onto the porch, then paused to
either side of the door.

Three officers ran around the side of the house, on
their way to the back door. I thought about the cus-
tomers inside. I thought about Corinne and silently
hoped she was on a bus pulling into the Greyhound
Station in Tucson, Arizona.

As a sixth or seventh patrol car raced down Garfield and crossed in front of me, its red lights flashed
through the cab of Paul's pickup. It occurred to me
why the officers were rushing the house. Marco
Morelli had escaped.

And Marco Morelli, I knew in my chilled bones,
wore the gun that the police ballistics lab could identify as the gun that fired the fatal shot into Paul Valley's
head.

I decided to drive away before the people inside
Rosalinda's got the chance to tell the officers about the
pickup truck with the camper. About the shotgun
blasts. The Kansas City, Kansas, cops would call Lieutenant Felker once they got around to opening the

trunk. The Metro Squad would take it from there. Lieutenant Felker would be looking for Rosalinda's punk brother before the sun was up.

I'd find him before Lieutenant Felker did was my hunch.

Chapter 23

Behind a closed grocery store, I stuffed the sheets and blanket in a Dumpster. I tucked in the surgical gloves I'd worn to and from the 800 block of Garfield Street, then returned to my apartment building.

I pulled my Datsun from my covered parking slot and backed Paul's pickup in, placing the bumper of the Ford against the concrete retaining wall. Inside my apartment I hurriedly packed clothes into two suitcases. I changed shoes. In the bathroom I loaded toilet articles into a soft-leather shoulder bag. I also packed my tools, an extra pair of skin-thin surgical gloves. I added some personal effects, the pictures of my mother and of Avery. And all the savings account passbooks. I stuffed the rest of the bag with clean towels.

I didn't have the heart to look into my other room, my broken studio. I'd start fresh one day.

In the front room I turned the easy chairs upright and placed my bag in one. I pushed my small couch back onto its four legs. I set the suitcases by the door. In the kitchen I found a bottle of vodka that had belonged to some girl who'd spent the night with me occasionally a few years ago. It was half empty.

A liquor bottle was never "half full," albeit your philosophical bent, because it only got emptier. I had yet in my lifetime to see one grow more full. I grabbed a cold beer from the fridge and carried it with the vodka into the bedroom. I sat down on the edge of the stripped bed and took a swig of vodka. I popped the top on the beer and drank down half of it. Beer cans, too, were never half full.

I dialed a bunch of numbers off the top of my head and waited.

"Carolyn?" I said into the phone. "Are you alone?"

"The question is whether I'm awake," her sleepy voice replied. "Alton?"

"Find some paper and something to write with. It's important."

"Just a minute," she mumbled.

Half empty, half full? My soul was barren. My body ached.

I gave her two phone numbers to write down, numbers I'd memorized from Lieutenant Warren Felker's business card. I told her to write down his name.

"Why?"

"Are you alone?"

"Alton!" Her voice singsonged in protest.

"It's important, Carolyn. Are you alone?"

"No, I'm not. It's Friday night and—"

"Good," I said, cutting her off.

I took another swallow of the clear vodka and wiped my mouth with the sleeve of Paul's satiny blue jacket. I chased it with more beer.

"Alton?"

"Paul's dead," I said clearly. It came out as two simple words that couldn't be misunderstood.

"What?"

"Paul's dead." It was the only way I could think to say it. "Carolyn, I'm sorry. He showed up unexpectedly and two men mistook him for me. They shot him, thinking he was me. I didn't know Paul was in town until I found him dead."

I paused. She didn't say anything. I couldn't even hear her breathe.

"The phone numbers are of the man who has his body. They caught one of the guys who killed him. . . ." I paused. There was no reason to go into that, just as there was no reason to tell Carolyn that Paul might have been killed out of spite once Norman Purdy and Marco Morelli were convinced he wasn't me.

"Carolyn?"

She cleared her throat. "Yes?" Her voice was a weak whisper.

"His dad lives in South Carolina. You know all that?"

"I won't go to the funeral, Alton," she announced from out of nowhere. I knew what she was saying. "I'll call this man and tell him to call Paul's dad, but I'm not going back with the body. I couldn't . . . I can't . . ."

Carolyn wasn't crying, but she couldn't talk. It sounded as if she were choking on a piece of something, a piece of terrible news.

"I'll come to Wichita," I promised her, "as soon as I can."

"Alton, come now. I'll wait up for you. Come now."

"I wish I could," I said, telling the truth. "But I can't. I have to do something first. It might take a day or two. It might be Monday or Tuesday before I can show up. Carolyn, are you all right?"

This time I could hear her breathing and nothing else.

"Be careful," Carolyn said solemnly. "I need you to stay alive."

"So do I." I waited for her to hang up. And even though the line went dead, I could hear Carolyn begin to weep. I threw the vodka bottle against the dresser. It shattered. I hoped Ray Sargent enjoyed listening to his recording of that phone conversation.

I went into the living room and sat in one of the chairs to think things through. The rope, the hammer, the pulleys. And the nails. Marco Morelli was on the run. Right where I wanted him.

I don't know how long I sat there. The security buzzer brought me out of a deep-thought stupor. Someone was ringing my apartment from the outer door. I could have risen to my feet and pushed the button on my callbox to find out who it was. Or I could have pressed the button that unlocked the security door to the building. I did neither, praying it was someone wanting someone else.

It sounded again. Ray Sargent, I decided, could press all the apartment buttons until someone let him in. He could play the national anthem on that buzzer and I wouldn't get up out of my chair.

Just in time I remembered that it could be possible that Marco Morelli was looking me up already. Not that it was likely. I jumped up and rushed to the sliding-glass doors. I opened them and stepped out onto my balcony. I couldn't see the door to the building from my balcony, but it didn't matter. They were already in the hallway.

Then someone was knocking on my unlocked apartment door, calling my name. One of my names.

"A-ver-ry! A-ver-ry! Please open the door."

I would have, but she tried the knob and found it unlocked. I was standing in the middle of the room in Paul's blue jacket when the door opened and Wynona Krebs lunged in. She wore a bright-red peasant blouse, down over both shoulders, her tightest blue jeans, and her cowboy boots. Only her hat was missing.

She stopped when she saw me, her hand on the door.

"Oh, A-ver-ry!"

"Shut the door," I directed.

I sat back down in the chair. Wynona closed the door. She stared down at my suitcases for the longest time, then looked up at me. Her eyes were reddened.

"I misshed you, A-ver-ry," she wailed. Wynona was drunk. "Why won't you see me no more?"

I thought of a million reasons. The only thing a woman understands when a man is leaving her is the presence of another woman in that man's life. It's the only thing that makes sense. Any other reason I could have come up with would have been either confusing or cruel.

"Rose is back," I confessed. "She just showed up."

"Rose?"

"I've been in love with her forever, Wynona. She was the one for me, you understand that?"

Wynona listened.

"When she dumped me, I went crazy. I was just getting things together when we met. You were good for me, Wynona. But . . . well . . . you know, Rose is back."

"She'll leave you again," Wynona declared. "A woman's either true or she ain't."

"It doesn't matter. She's my Juliet."

"Oh, A-ver-ry, don't you mish me?"

"Yes, yes, I do. But it doesn't matter."

"I understand. I'm going to mish you for a long, long time."

I nodded.

"The good men are always taken," Wynona insisted. "Can I shay good-bye, A-ver-ry?" As she asked this, Wynona Krebs unhooked her cowboy mother-of-pearl belt buckle.

"No," I said, holding up my hand. "There isn't time. She's waiting for me now." It occurred to me as I said it that Rosalinda probably *was* waiting for me. She'd rolled over in her sleep and had found me missing by now.

"There's always time for good-bye. You owe me that mush."

The door opened behind her and another voice joined the conversation.

"Sit down somewhere, Miss Krebs," Ray Sargent's gravelly voice intoned. He held his gun in front of him as a blind man holds his cane.

It was a regular convention. I should've had programs printed.

Wynona found the empty chair. I put my feet up

on the coffee table I would leave behind with the rest of the junk that cluttered my apartment.

"Rick," Wynona was saying, "you promised we'd be alone. You shaid you'd give me time!" Wynona was upset.

"I lied, Miss Krebs," Ray Sargent said harshly. He'd also lied about his name.

"Be quiet, Wynona," I told her. "Rick here tells lies, but his aim is true." Wynona pouted, too drunk to be frightened by something as small as a .32 automatic.

"Can I get anybody anything?" I offered, standing up. Hell, it was my castle we were in and I was king. Ray Sargent wasn't going to shoot anybody. But the barrel of his gun did follow my progress as I walked toward the kitchen.

"Me-eeeh," Wynona called.

I came back with two beers, the last of a twelve-pack. I handed one to Wynona and sat back down in my chair, feet up.

"You planning a little trip?" Ray Sargent asked me, pointing his gun at my suitcases.

"Rose is back," Wynona tried to explain to him for my benefit. She popped the top of her beer with a clumsy jerk, giggling as it foamed over into her lap. Wynona bent her mouth to the can to catch the overflow. Somebody, at least, was having fun.

"Your expenses are covered, I hope?" the ex-cop continued.

"Not yet," I said.

Ray Sargent kicked over my suitcases and, with the .32 still aimed in my general direction, stooped down to open them. He was visibly disappointed, one suitcase after the other, to discover they contained only clothes. And a pair of almost-new shoes.

The silver-haired security consultant stood up and looked around the room. He motioned to the travel bag sitting in my front room's third chair. I reached across the space between the two chairs and grabbed it by the strap. I set it on my lap and unzipped it down the middle. I pulled out the towels and held the bag open for his inspection.

Ray Sargent stepped forward and only glanced toward the bag. There wasn't enough room in the entire piece of small luggage to hold four hundred thousand dollars in cash.

"Tell me something, Sargent," I said.

He lifted his eyebrows, wrinkling the leathery skin of his face. His neatly trimmed mustache bristled.

"How much?"

He stared at me blankly, as if he were considering a chess move.

"You know the amount," I continued. "You were there. It was part of your job. So tell me, how much?"

I waited. I sipped from my beer. Ray Sargent didn't want to give in this easily. He wasn't ready to fully accept that I didn't have the money yet, that I wasn't on my way to pick it up without him.

"You said you'd call me," Wynona moaned from her chair.

"Shut up," I demanded. "Come on, Sargent, you may as well tell me if I'm the one who's going to find it for you. How much?"

"How much what?" Wynona wanted to know.

"I told you to shut up," I said.

"Five hundred eighty," Ray Sargent said. Wynona was standing up.

"I told you, Rick," she lamented. "Rose ish back!"

"She sure is, honey," Ray Sargent growled. He replaced his gun inside his jacket and smiled at me. It wasn't a cheerful smile. "The money's in town, Rooster," he announced.

"Maybe I'll wait till Christmas to give a good look for it," I said.

"Maybe," he said, taking Wynona by the arm. He opened the door and pushed Wynona outside. She giggled.

"Bye-bye, A-ver-ry. I mish you."

"I mish you too, doll," I called after her. Ray Sargent walked out without saying a word. "Same to you, friend," I said to the door as it closed behind him. The money was a real amount now. Half a million bucks. Plus. Eighty thousand dollars plus. I'd have settled for less. I'd have settled for killing Marco Morelli and letting it go at that.

Or so I told myself.

Chapter 24

Two bare feet could be seen in Rosalinda's window from the street. I locked my suitcases in the cab of the Datsun. I carried my shoulder bag over one arm, having added a box of .12-gauge shells to my personal effects. Under my other arm I toted the shotgun inside its slipcover.

Standing between her building and the Boy Scouts of America, I stared up at Rosalinda's feet. They didn't move. The window was open. There were a number of cars on the wet streets. One of them could have brought Marco Morelli to his sister's place. A cab could have pulled up and dropped him off.

At the end of Rosalinda's hallway I took the shotgun from inside its cover. A shell rested in the firing chamber. I approached her door ready to fire.

Rosalinda's door was unlocked and I didn't see any reason to knock. I turned the knob with my free hand, threw open the door, and jumped inside like a trained member of a SWAT team. There wasn't a sound inside the apartment. All I heard was my own breathing. Rosalinda's cat scooted out of the room and disappeared into the kitchen.

The lights weren't on. A lighted cigarette glowed in the ashtray. Rosalinda's feet were silhouetted in the window. She was lying on the bed on her back, her legs crossing the gap from the bottom of the window to the edge of her bed. She didn't turn to look at me.

"I'm alone," Rosalinda said, "if that's what you want to know."

A car drove by on the street below, making a strange swishing sound on the wet pavement. I let the bag slide from my shoulder. I pumped the shotgun five times in rapid succession. I picked up the live ammunition and walked through her apartment without saying anything.

I sat the live shells on the kitchen table, came back to the bed, and put down the shotgun beside it. I walked around to the other side of her bed and sat down by Rosalinda's outstretched legs.

I watched out the window, beyond her toes. My right hand massaged her knees.

"I love you," Rosalinda said.

"Norman Purdy is dead. He tried to shoot it out with the police over on the Kansas side."

"I love you," she repeated, afraid that what I was about to say would cause her never to speak to me again, to get up and walk into the kitchen and come back with a knife.

"Your brother got away."

"You set them up?"

I nodded in the semidarkness. I could feel her blue-diamond eyes on my back. "The whorehouse," I began, "on Garfield Street—"

"I don't want to know about it."

"They caught 'em with the body," I continued, leaving out the details. "The police will know if it was Norman Purdy's gun. If it wasn't his, then your brother's gun fired the bullet into Paul's head. Lieutenant Felker will know by morning."

"But you already know, don't you?" Rosalinda's voice came from a very distant part of her. I stopped rubbing her knees, rubbing my chin instead.

"And so do you," I said. There was nowhere to turn but to each other. This time I made love to Rosalinda and let the Boy Scouts of America catch an eyeful.

Rosalinda came like a freight train through the middle of the house at three in the morning. All her bones trembled and shook. Her lip quivered. She clutched at me so tightly I thought I might not continue to breathe. But I would not, could not, stop. Her feral odor flared my nostrils.

Rosalinda called out my name, making a breathless chant of it. Then her white teeth bit into the full, pink flesh of her lower lip and I placed my mouth there to feel the tension of her tongue. It tingled. And she cried out again, the voice of a bird trapped in her sweat-slickened chest, cried out at the beautiful agony of knowing that she was about to give it all up.

And I answered her cries with cries of my own because I could no longer contain it. Because I was weeping inside. Because my tears were falling onto the curved surfaces of her upturned face. We washed ourselves with our love, we bathed each other with our heartache. We soaked each other inside the flaming heat of our passion. And outside of the thrashing, clinging animal we'd become was locked our fear and loneliness of being alive.

I pulled her body up inside my arms, her mouth wet against my shoulder. Warm against my shoulder. Rosalinda bit into the skin of my shoulder to let me know she was there. Her arms held me locked against her, as did her glistening legs, as we rocked ourselves into oblivion.

"I love you, I love you," she sighed. She wept. I felt the heat of her burning words on my bitten skin. And then she hated me. "How can you do this to me? Damn you. Damn you, Alton. Damn you . . ."

In the morning we talked of Matisse. We talked about the faceless blue figures of Rosalinda's recent work. We talked about the fact that my suitcases were downstairs in the Datsun.

"We could leave together," Rosalinda suggested,

snuggling her cool cheek against the rooster tattooed on my chest. "We could leave today. I could get some money from my grandfather. We could," she insisted quietly, "if we wanted to."

"I can't run away," I said to the cat at the foot of Rosalinda's bed.

We held each other for the longest time. There was the sound of moving cars on Locust. Car doors opened and banged closed in the parking lot across the street: parents dropping their Boy Scouts off for whatever Saturday outing was scheduled. Their voices sounded like the voices of foreigners.

"Alton?"

"Hmmm."

"What do you want?"

I thought about that for a while.

"Two things," I said after some consideration. Rosalinda lifted her sweet face from the surface of my chest, offering me her undivided attention. "I want time to stop," I went on. "I want to hold you forever. And I want time to hurry up. I want this all to be over."

"What about the money?" Rosalinda rested her face against me again. "Do you want the money?"

"Finding the money, or at least finding out where the money went, is how this thing ends."

"But do you *want* it? Do you want it real bad?"

"No. It's not the money any longer. It hasn't been the money for a long time."

"What then, revenge?"

"Something like that. I want Paul's murderer to have to answer for killing him. I want him to know that . . ." I paused. I didn't know how to put it.

"You want him to know what?" Rosalinda encouraged me.

"I want him to know that . . . someone . . . that people loved Paul. That you can't kill someone and walk away from it. That you don't kill people for sport."

Rosalinda sighed heavily. "That's what this is all about, isn't it?"

I didn't say anything. My eyes were closed. Rosalinda's cat was staring at me with far too much concentrated curiosity.

"It's some sort of sport among men," she continued. I couldn't argue with that. "There are rules. And handicaps. And somebody wins—"

"Nobody wins," I corrected her.

"But somebody loses. We all lose, don't we? You play this game, and when it's over, you stand back and count up your losses."

There was nothing to say. That was one way of looking at it.

"Am I one of your losses?" Rosalinda wanted to know.

"True love is the devil's lunch box," was all I could think to say. It wasn't the right thing.

We were silent for some time, then Rosalinda asked me if I could see two birds she'd spotted outside the window. They sat close to each other, the two gray birds, on a telephone line.

"Those two birds are happy with each other," she said. "Why can't we be happy?"

I didn't say anything.

"Everybody wants what they can't have," she went on. "And to not be able to have something makes you want it all that much more, doesn't it? You never quit wanting something. . . . What those birds want is what they already have."

I rubbed my hand along her bare spine, listening.

"How come two birds in the wild mate for life?"

"Nobody lives happily ever after," I said.

"But everyone lives," she insisted. "Everyone gets a chance."

"Birds aren't people . . . they're . . . well, they're stupid . . . uh . . ."

"That's right, they're stupid little birds. And they're happy. Why can't we, if we're so damn smart, why can't we figure out a way to be happy with whatever we have or don't have?"

Rosalinda laughed.

"You know," she continued, "every once in a while we should be happy just to look at the sky. Not every day maybe, but once in a while we should just be happy to exist in the middle of all this wonder."

"You make me happy," I finally said. "Want to go sit on a wire somewhere?"

Later, when I was in the tub, Rosalinda stood in the doorway and asked me questions I didn't have the answers to. I told her I had to see Marco.

"Face-to-face," I said. "I have to make him look at this terrible thing he has done."

"Will you kill him?"

"I want to look in his eyes and ask him if he killed Paul. If he killed Dewey Boone and Lamar. I want him to know that he has to stop. You don't get to go around killing people to make your life interesting."

"You just want to kill him. You want to get even. But in the end he'll just be dead if you kill him. The score won't be tied. He'll just be dead and I'll be the one you hurt."

"I'll kill him only if he makes me kill him. It's necessary that I confront him."

"You have no choices as you see it?"

"None."

She eventually decided that she would help me, but insisted on being there. I wasn't too sure I liked the idea.

"Promise you won't shoot him."

"No promises. If he's disarmed—"

"That's some stupid rule you're making up! Oh, Alton, I want to be there. I'll help you if I can be there. I have to hear it too. I have to know too. Don't you see?"

"I don't know."

"If I can be there, I'll help you. That's the rule. If you don't let me help you, I'll hurt you. I'll keep it from happening. I'll warn him. I'll keep him away."

She was serious.

"Okay," I said. It would be easier with Rosalinda's

help. Without her help it could take me weeks to find a way to confront Marco Morelli on my terms. "But there's one more thing."

"I'm not the marrying kind," Rosalinda said, smiling at me.

"Part of the reason I love you," I quipped. "But that's not it. I want to meet the boss. I want to meet the Big Man. I want to meet your grandfather."

"You're on your own. And don't think talking to him will change the way the world works."

Chapter 25

We rigged Rosalinda's studio with the rope, the pulleys, the hammer, and the nails. She'd left a message for Marco where she knew he would receive it. He'd be coming soon. While we waited, I practiced with the Polaroid, taking Rosalinda's picture.

"How did you think of the rope?"

"My high school was too small to put together a football team," I explained. "If you weren't tall enough to play basketball, you messed around with rodeo."

"And with robbing grocery stores?"

"Something like that."

It could have been hours—but it wasn't. In fact, Marco showed up sooner than I'd expected. As Rosalinda and I had agreed, I was unarmed. She was certain that her brother wouldn't shoot me with her there. I wasn't so sure, but it didn't matter. One step inside the studio door and he was mine, all mine.

The lights were off and it was rapidly growing dark outside. Rosalinda had lighted two large candles, which she told me was not uncommon for her. Still,

Marco knew something was up. He knocked on the door without first trying the knob.

"Rose?" he called. "You alone?"

Rosalinda stood behind the couch. Her hands clutched at it as if it were a raft and she were drowning in a violent sea.

"Marco?" Rosalinda called in return, inviting him to come on in. And he did.

The human eye distinguishes as many as forty shades of gray. All that I could see clearly was shadow as the door opened and Marco Morelli waltzed inside Rosalinda's studio, inside my trap. Glistening in the shadow was the polished steel of a pistol barrel held in front of him.

I pulled the rope from my position behind the door, rapidly drawing up the loop that encircled his feet. I put my full weight behind it and charged like a horse in the opposite direction, jerking his swagger out from under him and lifting his heels toward the high ceiling.

I felt the weight of Marco's body as he was yanked from his footing to hang upside down from the pulley bracketed to the support beam of the ceiling. I heard his weapon clatter to the floor and was delighted by the sound.

Rosalinda turned on the lights. I secured the rope to a bracket I had nailed to the opposite wall.

"What the hell is this?" Morelli hissed. "Haunted house?"

Rosalinda didn't say anything. She also didn't look at her brother hanging upside down inside the door. Mark tested the strength of his trap by kicking with both legs, causing his body to swing.

"Careful," I said, picking up his gun. "The blood is already rushing to your head. You get too dizzy and you're liable to throw up on yourself."

"You promised," Rosalinda pleaded, meaning the gun. I hadn't realized I was pointing it at him.

It was a .45 automatic. A hand cannon. It wasn't the weapon I'd expected her brother to be carrying.

I'd anticipated that he'd still have on him the .32, the murder weapon. Maybe he was smarter than I'd given him credit.

Marco's face was flushed. I studied him momentarily, turning the gun away. His eyes were mean and gray, a shade nearer silver than Rosalinda's pure blue eyes. He looked like a kid snatched from the playground. In fact, that was the idea that stole my thoughts: children.

Rosalinda and her brother were children. I was the only adult in the room, it seemed.

She sat on the couch now, glancing at her brother, writhing her hands and biting her lip. Mark breathed heavily with his mouth held open. He looked like a wet cat. His leather jacket was bunched against his chin.

The .45 bothered me. What if I'd been wrong? If this was the weapon Marco usually carried, then he hadn't shot Dewey and Lamar Boone. He hadn't assassinated Paul.

"You want the money, Rooster," the little creep was saying, "you got the wrong person."

"I got the right person," I said, reassuring myself. It couldn't have been Ray Sargent all along. I couldn't have been that wrong about everything. "Quit squirming around and keep your goddamned mouth shut."

"You want the money, ask her," he shot back. "Ask Rose."

I walked to him and placed the barrel of the .45 an inch from his forehead, where his eyes could fix on the black, round opening. I heard Rosalinda gasp. Marco's eyes strained to see beyond the gun, to look at me to see if I was going to pull the trigger. Beads of sweat broke out on his forehead.

"You," I told him, "are allowed to breathe. Nothing more."

He took a deep breath and closed his eyes.

"Take our picture," I said to Rosalinda. "Take a close-up of the pistol to your brother's head."

She hesitated. "Hurry!" I demanded. "My finger itches."

Rosalinda did as she was told. The resulting snapshot showed Marco Morelli's eyes open wide in what might be interpreted as terror, particularly when one noted the presence of the gleaming barrel of an automatic sticking out of his upside-down ear. I placed the picture on the table.

"What now?" Marco asked. "You going to unzip my pants?"

Rosalinda's presence gave him strength. It was as if he knew no harm would come to him while she was in the room.

"No," I hissed in anger. "I'm going to use your head for a football, and I'm going to kick your brains through the goalposts."

"Alton," Rosalinda said to get my attention. I didn't turn to look at her. "Marco," she said, shifting tactics, "keep your mouth shut for a minute."

There was a tremor of fear in her voice.

"Look, Rose," he protested, "if Rooster wants the money, I ain't got it—"

"He doesn't want the money," she snapped. "He wants you."

There was a silence between them. I couldn't help but notice an electricity as they looked upon each other's face. Rosalinda looked as if she were about to collapse, as if only the torment of the situation kept her standing.

Tears of confusion stained her ashen cheeks.

"And whose side are you on, little sister?"

"Yours," she said. "He'd have killed you already if I weren't here."

"And you think all you have to do is smile and he'll let me go?"

"I . . ." Rosalinda paused. Then more firmly she said, "I don't know."

I was thinking about Ray Sargent. About his .32 automatic. About Paul's blood-soaked Hawaiian shirt. I was thinking seriously about blowing Marco Morelli's face into oblivion. The act might, I thought, clear up my confusion.

"You killed Dewey Boone," I shouted. "You killed Lamar Boone for no reason at all except that he was there. And you killed my best friend in cold blood. You listened to him beg for his life and then you shot him in the head."

Mark's body tensed. "Hey," he said lamely, "you got the wrong guy."

"No!" I roared ferociously. "*You* got the wrong guy!

"Alton, don't!" Rosalinda screamed.

I realized my knuckles were white, locked tightly around the grip of Marco's .45. I was moments from squeezing off one or two quick rounds. My finger on its own had made up its mind to blast a bee of burning lead through one of his eyes. When Rosalinda screamed, I managed to turn away from him.

She sat on the couch, the devastation of her emotional dilemma clear in the stare of her blue eyes. She buried her hand between the cushions of the couch. The gesture made no sense to me.

When I turned back around, her brother's face was beet red.

"You'll bleed to death hanging upside down," I calmly informed him. "The capillaries in your nose will eventually burst and you'll either bleed to death or drown in your own blood."

Marco tried in vain to lift himself from the waist. His stomach muscles were too weak.

I leaned against the table and Rosalinda relaxed a little.

"You know, I've seen your face before," I told the hanging goon. "I've seen it in prison a hundred times. You're violent and you're evil and you're never going to change. I'd be doing your family a favor if I put you away, Marco." I mocked Rosalinda's voice as I said his name.

I hoped some of what I was saying was having an impact on Rosalinda. Marco was beyond convincing.

"You're dangerous scum and you don't fool me for a moment."

I let it sit for a while.

"He's going to kill me, Rose!" Marco suddenly blurted out.

"Shut up!" I said. Rosalinda tensed.

"I *want* to kill you, Marco," I confessed. "And all you have to do is cooperate. All you have to do is hang there and say the wrong thing. All you have to do is tell me one more lie. And you're dead."

It was true that I wanted to hurt him. I wanted him to be in pain. I wanted him to feel some kind of anguish. Rosalinda's presence was, in fact, protecting him from my rage.

"Where's your grandfather?"

"You can't touch the old man," Marco bragged. "Besides, he has nothing to do with this."

"Tonight," I ordered. "Where is he tonight? Where is he right now?" I stood up from leaning against the table, the .45 in my hand.

"Bowling," Marco said quickly. "Saturday night, he bowls."

"Where?"

"Mission, Mission Bowling Alley. He owns the place, has it close down Saturdays. It's off Johnson Drive."

"Thank you," I said sarcastically. I turned away from him, wishing there were a screw I could tighten into his guts. It wasn't enough that he squirmed. I laid the gun on the table with Rosalinda's paper and paints. I kept my hand on it and tried to steady my nerves.

"Notice," I said to Rosalinda, "that your brother forgot to deny killing Paul. Take note of that." It may have been unnecessarily cruel of me to have said that, but it was beginning to dawn on me that I wouldn't kill him.

Marco Morelli was a piece of slime. He hurt other people. He killed for the hell of it; but despite Paul's murder, I couldn't shoot an unarmed man. I couldn't bring myself to kill the helpless creature even if tomorrow I was certain he would not be helpless again.

Rosalinda screamed. It was the wild scream of a wild creature.

I spun partially around and saw her standing from the couch, a piece of silver jewelry in her hand. I heard the pop of a gun and watched the orange flame leap from her hand like a tongue from a lizard's mouth. Another gun was firing.

The window across the room shattered. I turned around and saw that Marco had taken a bullet in his arm. The lucky shot had caused him to lose his grasp on the .32 automatic that had been inside his leather jacket all along.

Rosalinda was in shock. I picked up Marco's gun. She stood frozen in place. I had the murder weapon in my hand, pointed at Marco's cringing face. Blood splattered on the wooden floor, dripping from his wound.

When I looked up, Rosalinda's small gun was pointed at me. Our eyes locked. Hers were full of tears and pain. I dropped the gun. She'd saved my life.

I took the small-caliber pistol from Rosalinda's hand. It was a purse-size .25 with a silver-etched body and mother-of-pearl grips. It *was* a piece of jewelry, a gift no doubt from her grandfather or from her father a number of years ago. She'd had it tucked under the couch cushion.

"He did it." She wept. "He did it, didn't he?"

"Yes," I said, holding her. "I'm sorry."

Chapter 26

I held the .45 to Marco's head while I wrapped his fingers around the .32 that had been used to murder Dewey and Lamar Boone. That had been used to fire the fatal bullet into Paul Valley's head. Only Marco's fingerprints were now on the .32. They'd nail him for one of those murders if not all three. I had faith in Lieutenant Felker.

Downstairs, Rosalinda called an ambulance. Then she called Felker. Her story was that Marco had shown up in a rage, that he'd attacked her and that she'd shot him in self-defense. The harassment complaint would substantiate her story. The fact that Marco's weapon had been fired wouldn't hurt any.

I was fairly certain that no state charges would be pressed against Rosalinda. Marco wouldn't press his own charges against her; Granddad would have his head on a prison platter if he tried.

I took down my rigging, careful to keep an eye on Marco. He stared at me from the couch, masking his pain, his hands tied behind his back. I had nothing to say to him.

Rosalinda held her gun on her brother as I loaded everything, including the .45 automatic, into my Datsun pickup. I tried to come up with something to say that would be of comfort to her. I could never imagine what she was feeling, but I knew it had to be awful. I had also never imagined that I'd end up loving her quite so much.

Parked near the end of the block, I watched the ambulance arrive a full two minutes behind the police. I watched the uniformed figures move inside the studio, walking toward the windows, then walking away.

I wondered what they thought of Rosalinda's faceless paintings.

Convinced that Marco Morelli was being taken into custody, I drove away. There was someone I was in a hurry to meet. I had a photograph in my pocket to show him.

As I drove the Datsun straight on Thirty-ninth Street, I spotted him following me for the first time. He had to step on it to keep from losing me at the light. I circled a four-block area before reaching Mission Road to be certain.

I pulled into a car wash at Forty-seventh and Mission. I parked my pickup in one of the bays and walked out to the street. The '84 Camaro sat in a closed filling station half a block away. I waved to him. The rented car's headlights flashed on, then off.

I ended up in the passenger's seat.

"Where we headed?" Ray Sargent asked, giving notice to but not staring at the .45 automatic I pointed in the direction of his sixty-year-old belly.

"To hell," I answered flippantly, but my reply hung in the air like a cloud of doom. "I just wanted you to know that you may be right."

"About what?"

"Morelli. They've arrested him for the murder of Paul Valley."

"What about the girl?" Ray Sargent smelled a rat.

"What about her?"

"She tell you where the money is?"

"The money's gone," I told him with a straight face. "Dewey ditched it. Maybe his sister's sitting on it. I don't care about that."

Ray Sargent shut off the engine. "You don't care about it now," he said, turning in the seat to face me, "but you will. It'll eat at you until you're a nervous wreck. You'll come back for it. Or you'll start all over again and try and rip off another bank. I know you, Rooster."

"Maybe."

"If you think his sister's the key, I can help you. If

you think Dewey left it somewhere where she can find
it, we can find it first."

"What if she's already got it?"

"She doesn't," Ray Sargent said flatly. In the semidarkness his voice sounded like the voice of an animal.
"I've been keeping my eye on that angle."

Animals, I thought. Lions and tigers and bears.
And Ray Sargent. Wild animals. I was walking through
the woods surrounding the yellow brick road. The gun
in my hand was the courage, the brains, the heart I
needed to deal with the threatening shadows that cluttered my progress.

"I'm on my way to see the old man," I told him.
"You want to come along?"

"Damn!" Ray Sargent exclaimed, ignoring my re-
mark. He slapped the steering wheel with his right
hand. "I knew she had it. I just knew it. Are you sure,
Rooster? Are you sure Rosalinda didn't buffalo you?"

"I'm sure. . . . You want to come along?"

"What for? What good will it do to confront him?
You think there's somebody keeping score? You think
you'll win something worthwhile by telling her grandfather off?"

"Well?" I waited for him to say yes or no.

"I'd rather find the money."

I opened the passenger's door a crack and the
dome light came on. Ray Sargent's leathery face appeared older in the yellow light. He looked helpless.
He looked handcuffed to the place where he sat, the
tattoo on his hand fading further.

"I'm sorry, Rooster. But this is something you
have to do. Not me."

"Right again," I chirped. Then I remembered
that Ray Sargent had something I wanted. I lifted the
.45 in pure mean-spiritedness. "One more thing."

Ray Sargent cocked his head and opened his eyes
wide to consider my request.

"My daughter. You said you know where she is."

The retired cop rubbed his mustache. He was either weighing the cost of not telling me or considering

the ramifications of telling me a lie. Or maybe he couldn't remember. Or maybe he'd made it up in the first place. My heart raced.

"Louisville," he finally said. "Her name is Turpin. T-U-R, P-I-N."

"I've been there," I said without emotion. I pushed open the door and climbed out. I turned around as I walked away to see that he was watching me, that the passenger's door was still open. I waved. At least someone would know if I didn't come back.

I hummed along with "Puff the Magic Dragon" as I drove south on Mission Road. As I crossed over on Sixty-third. As I drove two blocks of Johnson Drive and turned left on a yellow light. I pulled into the parking lot of the Mission Bowl on Martway.

I patted my shirt pocket to make certain the snapshot of Marco hanging upside down with a .45 to his head was still there. It was. I put on a fresh pair of latex surgical gloves. I checked the clip in the .45 to find it carrying a full complement of ammunition.

The exterior and lobby lights of the bowling alley were out. Leon Morelli had it all to himself.

I parked across the street and watched two burly guys come out the glass doors, fat guys in cheap suits, bodyguards. Off to get a pizza no doubt. They pulled away in a limousine with tinted windows.

The lobby doors were left unlocked. I could hear pins falling as I stepped into the outer lobby. I thought I might have been doing this for me, getting to the top of the heap of organized garbage in Kansas City, the last livable city. But I might have been doing it for Rosalinda. Her heart was part my heart.

Perhaps, like her, I believed her grandfather was responsible for everything bad. For Dewey and Lamar's getting shot. For Rosalinda's father and my best friend's ending up murdered. For Norman Purdy's dying like a jerk in the spotlight of a police helicopter.

I expected my entry to be noticed and was prepared to defend myself. I carried the heavy automatic at my side.

Images tumbled through my mind as I walked along the red carpet, as I quietly and purposefully strode the length of the bowling alley toward the light that illuminated two men bowling on lane 24. Glimpses of Rosalinda's body, her face, her eyes. And there was Dewey Boone grinning confidently from behind the pool table at the student union, an unlighted cigarette dangling from his cocky sneer.

Paul's death-face. Carolyn's chagrined expression when I interrupted her making love. The girl in the yellow dress.

Norman Purdy gunned down by the cops. Marco Morelli hanging upside down. The chubby jailer in Madrigal, Oklahoma. Ray Sargent sitting in the chair in Lamar Boone's living room. The cuckoo clock. Rosalinda's ashen face and trembling lip as she held her gun on me after shooting her brother.

Dewey Boone's four fingers frozen in death. Corinne walking in from the motel bathroom. Dewey Boone's four fingers. Wynona Krebs standing naked in her elaborately decorated cowboy boots. Dewey Boone's sister nursing her child. Dewey Boone running up the hill with the gunnysack. Oleta Pryor passed out in the front seat of her compact station wagon. *Dewey's fingers.*

I expected someone to shout at me from the shadows. I pictured myself dropping to one knee and blowing away the lion, the tiger, the bear, behind the ball return machine. The lion, the tiger, the bear, standing up from behind the service counter. I sat down at a table behind the bowling area and lifted my gun to the tabletop.

The old man was bowling. He wore a brilliant white shirt and dark dress pants. White bowling shoes. He held a customized bowling ball colored with blue swirls. He studied the pins. He took a series of short, quick steps and stooping, brought the ball back and swung it forward.

The blue-swirled ball looked like a miniature planet earth as it rolled in a controlled curve toward the kingpin: a strike. Leon Morelli turned around, his right hand fisted, his elbow tucked in a self-congratulatory gesture. I was surprised to see that he wore glasses, black-framed glasses.

The old man looked seventy, big but not flabby. He picked up a can of beer and sat down in one of the seats behind the scorer's table. The other man was also fat, also not young. He was smoking a cigarette.

From behind it took me a moment to recognize Sam Geolas.

"You got to bend over, you want to bowl," the old man called after Geolas. He laughed at himself and drank more beer, obviously winning.

Geolas bowled stiffly, dropping the ball so that you were surprised it rolled forward. It took down three pins. His second ball fit into the gap the three pins had left. Sam Geolas was either losing on purpose or he'd never bowled before. He picked up his burning cigarette from the ashtray at the scorer's table and saw me.

It was time for the Big One. I shot him before he had a chance to sit down. The .45 blasted a round of lead into his left thigh, and Sam Geolas toppled over the scorer's table and fell to the floor. You could hear him curse in pain. You could see him writhe on the floor. He knew what had hit him.

The old man stood on the bowling floor, blinking at me from the other side of his corrective lenses, trying to find me in the shadows.

"Who is that?" Leon Morelli demanded in a loud, cranky voice. His voice echoed down the empty bowling hall.

"It ain't the cops, grandpa," I called to him.

Leon Morelli was in my sights, my arms resting on the table, my right hand holding the gun's butt, my left hand holding my right hand steady.

"I don't understand," he said. "Why did you shoot my friend? I want to know."

The old man could've thrown the ball at me. He

could have dropped to the floor. He could have made a run for it. Instead, he stood there, holding his sixteen-pound globe against his belly, wanting to know.

I squeezed the trigger. Again. Again. And once more.

The first slug hit the ball, exploding it into two rough halves that flew from Morelli's grasp. He fell backward with the impact, crying out. The remainder of the shots were in him before he hit the floor, ruining his white shirt. Leon Morelli's head rested in the gutter of lane 24.

I got up and walked to the bowlers' area to find Geolas sitting on the floor, his back against the seats. A song danced in my head, a song I couldn't remember the words to. It was the Stones. Geolas could see it in my eyes. Could see what I was about to do.

I ground out the cigarette butt he'd let drop to the floor. I got blood on my shoes. I put the gun to his head. I fired four times. Sam's blood splattered back on me; my gloved gun-hand appeared as if it had been used for major surgery.

"You run with the wrong crowd," I told the dead man.

I dropped the gun in his lap. Paul Valley always liked to bowl. And he should have been able to. I pulled off the gloves slowly, snapping the sticky fingers, turning them wrongside out. I threw them atop the pile of Sam's body at my feet. They'd think it was a professional hit.

But it was personal. The cops would never have gotten around to doing it.

Chapter 27

I drove home with a ringing in my ears. My heart raced. At the apartment building on Thompson Street I decided not to go home. Instead, I changed trucks, loading everything from my Datsun into Paul's battered Ford pickup. We'd come back for the Datsun later.

I drove through the Country Club Plaza. It was the prettiest of early-summer nights. Lights ignited the fountains. The sprays of water looked like fireworks. I drove up the Paseo. I crossed over to Broadway and drove between the tall hotels in downtown Kansas City, Missouri. I crossed the Mighty Mo, tossing my quarter into the plastic basket that winked a green light at me in return.

I should have been afraid of myself, but I wasn't. I should have disliked myself, but I didn't. I disliked the world, though.

Rosalinda would understand.

There'd been bad times in my life. There'd been times when I'd been convinced that inside every cloud was another cloud. I used to tell myself that this was the worst year of the rest of my life. The idea was that things would get better, the years would be better years. A person couldn't always be right.

I didn't feel like stopping. I needed the motion. I turned around at Kansas City International and drove back toward town. I rode with my suitcases up front. I rode with my Johnnie Walker Black. I drove in large circles, saying good-bye, with only one place really to go. Dewey's four fingers pointed the way.

I returned to the scene of the crime.

I parked where Dewey had parked. I climbed the hill topped with the row of blue oaks. Johnnie Walker came with me. I sat on the crest of the hill, having to clear a spot among the large acorns with the toe of my bloodstained shoe. Few cars moved on Nall Avenue below.

I heard him approaching, but I didn't turn to look. It would take him a minute or two to locate me. I waited. The sky was full of stars and off to the right you could see the pink glow of the city lights. Kansas City looked as if it were on fire. I waited, the stars watching, until he stood directly behind me.

I handed the bottle up over my shoulder. Ray Sargent took a drink and handed it back.

"You can put away the gun," I said. He slipped the .32 into the pocket of his jacket. Ray Sargent stepped around to stand at an angle, watching my face.

"Nice night," he said. "There's a breeze."

I'd grown to almost like the sound of his gravelly voice.

"Damn tall trees, aren't they?"

"Big as they come," he said.

"Like fingers pointing at something in the sky."

"I suppose," Ray Sargent allowed. The ex-cop wasn't one to wax poetic. But Dewey Boone was. We listened to the night that held us under the trees in shared communion. Then Ray threw back his head and laughed. He slapped his thigh.

"It's here, isn't it?"

I told him to keep it down, that he should be careful of his bad heart. His response was to laugh even more loudly. I smiled, in spite of the aching hole inside me.

"You took too long getting around to the other side of the hill," I explained. "He'd planned it all along. I don't know, maybe he was scared of carrying it. Maybe he realized that was where the risk was. . . ."

"Or maybe he didn't want the responsibility."

"Yeah, or maybe he was going to disappear for a couple weeks, come back, and ride off into the sunset with all of it."

The stars understood everything, including the

folly of our being there. The folly of our giving a damn about anything besides each other. All of us. The stars didn't occupy desolate places, it was the rest of us living inside ourselves.

"I feel like Gatsby," I told Ray Sargent.

"How's that?"

"I feel like my dream, the thing I was chasing, is already behind me and I've just discovered it."

"That's pretty good thinking for an Okie. But Rooster, a man's only as good as his dream." It sounded like something he'd read on a poster, but I knew what he meant.

"Then we need better dreams, you and I," I improvised.

"Well, what you need and what you get don't always come on the same train." Ray Sargent would have gotten along well with my mother.

I led Ray Sargent to the tree fourth in the direction from which Dewey Boone had approached the stand of trees atop the slender hill. Sometimes the truth slaps you upside the head like a brick tossed from a bus traveling at full speed. I could have been wrong. I could have been doubtful. However, I was certain that the money was there. All four bags.

Ray found it by brushing away a small pile of leaves at the base of the fourth tree. Under the leaves was a mound of fresh dirt covering a two-foot-by-two-foot plywood square. The piece served as the lid for the hole Dewey had dug one night after we'd finalized our plans for the robbery.

Ray lifted out the money bags. One at a time. A distant light, from a passing car perhaps, glinted off his handcuffs lapel pin and I thought to ask him about the small piece of jewelry.

"My heart's a little weak, Rooster. Looks like I'll only be able to carry two of these." There was no need to say anything more, no reason to ask questions. The sixty-year-old ex-cop lifted a money bag in each hand and turned to trudge down the hill to where he'd parked the rented Camaro. He stopped and gave me a good look over his shoulder. "You know," he said, "I never thought you'd come out of that bowling alley alive."

He disappeared into the darkness, carrying his retirement fund with him.

I finished off the Johnnie Walker. I'd counted that money in my head so many times that I was beginning to think that it belonged to me. I kicked clumsily at the two remaining money bags. Ray Sargent was as tough as a burnt two-dollar steak. I wasn't.

They say it's easiest to get away with murder. Love was something else entirely different. Rosalinda was something I'd never escape. The lights were on at her studio, but when I knocked on the door, no one answered. I looked inside to find nobody home.

On my way out, I noticed a piece of paper at my feet. Rosalinda had mounted the drawing of me and the horses on bristol board. She'd added a piece of red paper to the work. The red paper was torn into the shape of a tiny ragged heart. It covered half of my chest, where my rooster tattoo was cut into my skin. At the bottom of the picture she'd written in a precise hand: *What is lost between us will come up trees.*

I liked that. Rosalinda was as magical as I'd dreamed her inside my cage in Madrigal, Oklahoma. What was lost between us *would* come up trees, tall trees. Rosalinda had set me free. I wished I could say I'd done the same thing for her.

I drove to her apartment on Locust Street anyway, the sacks of money stuffed unceremoniously behind the seat of the Ford pickup; her work of art lay flat atop my suitcases. I parked on the street. I leaned against the hood of Paul's truck and stared up at her window, at the soles of her bare feet.

I pictured her blue eyes staring at the ceiling. I pictured her mouth parted slightly. I pictured her with me.

One day, I prayed, she'd have reason to smile at the thought of me. But it would be a while.

I saluted the Boy Scouts of America. I was about to do my good deed by getting back in Paul's pickup and driving away. In the morning they and Rosalinda would work out a way of getting through the rest of their lives. For me, there were two hundred miles of clean highway driving to help me beat back the blues. Maybe that song would come on the oldies station, the one I was always waiting for. Maybe Carolyn would decide to go to that funeral with me after all. And maybe I'd stop in Louisville on our way home.

Frank De Felitta, author of *Audrey Rose*, returns to print with a tale so chilling it must be heard to be believed, and once heard will never be forgotten.

FUNERAL MARCH
by Frank De Felitta

There's a serial killer loose on the streets of Los Angeles, a killer whose slayings are so bizarre the police are stumped. The only common factor: the murderer's seeming flair for showmanship. Without a pattern to tie the slayings together, Lieutenant Fred Santomassimo digs deeper into the madman's shadowy world, finding himself drawn into the often deceiving world of motion pictures. Here he will find the answers he's looking for, but the solution will be nothing like he expected....

Frank De Felitta's **Funeral March**. For some, the last tune they'll ever hear.

On Sale in March from Bantam Crime Line Books.

AN207 -- 2/91

BANTAM MYSTERY COLLECTION